The Shiloh Renewal

The Shiloh Renewal

Joan Leslie Woodruff

Black Heron Press
Post Office Box 95676
Seattle, Washington 98145

ISBN: 0-930773-50-0

Cover art: Deborah Mersky

Published by
  Black Heron Press
  Post Office Box 95676
  Seattle, Washington 98145

   Web Site: http://mav.net/blackheron

1

I was seventeen when I met the banshee. It came at me on a wind from Hell and swept me into a sea of decayed wars and souls too wounded to drift on.

2

If I'd had a stick I would've hit the woman who pulled the curtain shut. I wanted it left open so I could see the clock. Without the clock face speaking time to me, how would I know I was still alive?

I was cruising past angry, fresh out of a fuse, when a pudgy hand grasped the curtain and ripped it back. A nurse looked at the gurney my sister Penny lay on. She picked up my sister's arm and checked her pulse. "This one's dead," the nurse whispered.

I tried to sit up, but the right side of my body wouldn't work and my brain seemed to be twirling, burning in a sea of fire inside my head. I fell back, grabbed the rail of my sister's gurney with my left hand, and held it in a vice grip no one would break.

"The head injury's still with us," she seemed surprised.

A skinny nurse appeared at the first one's side. They stared at me. Skinny one said, "She's in shock."

"The dead one has to go to the basement, but the head injury won't let us move the stretcher. She'll be gone in a while, too. Can't understand how she can still be alive. Poor kids. Must've been one hell of an accident."

I tightened my grip on the gurney, fixed them with swollen scared eyes until they pulled the curtain shut. When they did, I couldn't see the clock. I wanted to scream out for them to open the curtain, but I had to be humble, had to get someone to help me and my sister.

I thought of the Great Spirit Magicians and the Miracle God.

I didn't know Who to ask. I'd never been good at religion. I'd never been good at much. My sister groaned. She wasn't dead. I wasn't going to let her be dead. She was my best friend. Neither of us were going to be dead. These people could pull their curtains so they wouldn't see us bleed and suffer, but we'd lay and wait and I'd figure out something.

My sister groaned again. I pulled on her gurney, rolled it closer to me, said "Hey! Don't let go!"

I knew the nurses didn't have the power to help us. They were simple people. Mortal flesh. I hadn't asked for their help, anyway.

My sister stopped groaning. She was very...quiet.

"Please God, please Great Spirits. I'll be good the rest of my life..."

The heavy nurse yanked the curtain open, poked her head in. I tried to look up at her, but I couldn't make my eyes work.

"She's still with us," the nurse said.

I gently tugged at my sister's blood soaked braids. She was too still.

I continued my prayer, "Help! Please help! I'll be good all the rest of my life.

"Is Anyone listening?

"I feel all alone.

"I think there are no Gods. There is only me, crushed like road-kill, and my sister slipping away, and a couple of people dressed in white who wish we'd go away so they could have their coffee break."

Then!

My sister muttered my name. I heard her say it.

She said my name! I reached, took her arm, held it tight. It was a miracle!

I prayed, "Thank You God and All Great Spirits for showing me a miracle. I'll be a perfect person. I promise. I'll do good things for every one. Thank You, thank You, thank You."

My sister's arm began to feel cold. I shook it. Pinched it. It seemed she wasn't breathing.

"Hey! God! Aren't You listening? What's the matter? Got too many other things to do?"

My sister's wrist twitched.

"I'm sorry, God. Smart mouth, You know. Sorry. You really are a very good Magician, making my sister be alive. After all she went through. That windshield. It was a mean thing for her to go through."

Someone snatched the curtain aside. I could see a bright light, nothing else. I heard wheels creaking. My hand flew out from my side. My sister's gurney was gone!

"Help!" I screamed.

"I'm taking you into surgery," a man said.

3

"How are we today, Miss Sandy!"

I struggled to open my eyes. In spite of its commanding pitch and piercing tone, the voice was kind. A strange man owned it. Not my father, an uncle, or any relation.

"Who are you?" I asked.

"Nurse!" he called out.

Peering from a narrow slit shadowed by my lashes, I forced one eye to look at him. I tried to control my hands, wanted to guide them to my face, feel around, discover what prevented me from using both eyes. My left hand wanted to respond, but my right arm ignored me and continued to rest heavily at my side.

"Yes, Doctor Rheis," a woman answered as she ran across what sounded like a linoleum floor.

"Who is that?" I asked.

"She's awake!" the woman seemed surprised—even shocked. "Bring me the neurological trauma kit," he barked.

"Hey! What's that?" I asked. I wasn't having any luck getting answers.

It was an interesting game we played with this something or other kit, especially when the doctor asked how many items were in the pictures he held before my face. My narrow slit of a peep-hole into the world offered less than a clear view. All was out of focus and there was more than one of everything. I tried to explain this to the doctor and nurse, but they raised their voices and talked over me. My energy failed me and I wanted to sleep. I pretended to snore, but forgot to close my eye.

"Doctor," the nurse gasped, "I think she's choking."

The doctor moved his face close to mine and I could see he was grinning. "She isn't choking," he chuckled. He was on to my trick. Then he left, taking the something or other kit with him. The nurse stayed behind to check my pulse and blood pressure, and stick a thermometer in my mouth.

When she was gone another woman came in to stare down at me. This woman was old, dressed in a floor-length black skirt and a billowy gingham blouse. A white pinafore, appearing to be stained with dark blood, hung loose down her front. Her hair was unadorned in a severe knot behind her head.

"They line the corridors wall to wall," she whispered. "It matters little now whether they wore Confederate grey or Federal blue when they arrived. I use the same cloth to wipe perspiration from their young faces. I don't think they mind, do you?"

I shook my head as best I could manage. "Some of them suffer terribly from their wounds. But in the end, they will probably die. I believe it's a blessing, considering their injuries."

I closed my eye and slept. When I awoke, she was gone.

My days continued similarly. I demonstrated the behavior and I.Q. of a log. Doctor Rheis used a sharp pin to prick my skin, always asking, "Did you feel that?" I never responded, but kept my eye upon his white coat, occasionally noting it was stained with blood, too. After the pins, he frequently held up his hand, asked how many fingers I could see. Again, it was senseless to respond. I tried to tell him before. I could see more than one of everything. He hadn't paid attention then, and I didn't see a need to give him a second chance.

Nurses were a bothersome talky bunch of people. They cruised in and out of my room whenever they pleased and spoke loudly in their know-it-all jargon. They were fond of saying things like: "Your cerebral edema is reducing," or "Your right body isn't as flaccid," or "Sometimes children heal quickly with little residual hemiplegia and neurological impairment."

Cerebral?

Flaccid?

Hemiplegia?

Neurological impairment?

What the hell kind of language was that? I figured they were trying to insult me, especially when they called me a child. I was hardly a child. My memory was fuzzy and frequently escaped me, but I believed my senior year of high school was ahead of me. As for their fancy fifty cent words, I didn't know what they meant. Wasn't sure I cared.

I did want to know where my sister was.

"Where is Penny?" I called out next time I saw a nurse cruising past my doorway.

"Blanche, come here a minute," the nurse said, addressing someone off my view screen. My left hand was working better now, which was good because I was left handed. I reached to my eye, used my fingers to stretch my lid wider.

"Her motor control's improving," the first nurse said to Blanche.

They both leaned over my bed. Blanche spoke first, "Do you think she's trying to say something, or do you think this is just incoherent babble?"

"I'm not trying to say something, I am saying something. What's wrong with your ears? Where is Penny!?"

"She thinks she is talking, that's the problem," the first nurse said. "I'm going to recommend Rheis prescribe speech therapy." She was glancing at her wristwatch. "Oh, it's five o'clock already! I've got to prepare the pill cart."

Blanche remained in my room, taking my pulse, filling my water glass, and finally, opening the shade across my window. I could hear her pulling a chair beside my bed.

"Go ahead, have a seat," I suggested. "Take a load off."

"I know you're frustrated," she said. "You've been in a coma for several weeks. I can't imagine what it's like being locked in a prison inside your own body. Head injuries are the worst injuries, but you've got the magic of youth on your side, and we're going to help you all we can."

"Fine! Bring my sister here! Now!"

Blanche reached over, patted my head. "There, there," she soothed, "calm down. We're going to get you an appointment with a speech therapist who will help you learn to talk again."

At that moment the old woman in the pinafore returned. She walked to my bedside, ignoring Blanche who sat at her elbow. "All hell has broken loose," the woman whispered. "This morning Lieutenant General Beauregard pulled out of Jackson. We are left undefended."

"What do you mean?" I asked.

"Johnston has dispatched Beauregard, and together they march toward Camp Shiloh."

I focused my eye on her cautiously and asked, "Are you talking to me?"

"Why, of course, dear girl. To whom else would I speak?"

Blanche seemed not to notice this woman. She got up from the chair and left my room.

"Listen," I said, "I need your help."

"What would you have me do?"

"Find my sister. Her name is Penny. She has long black hair and she wears a braid. I know she's here...she was here before."

"Before the war?"

"The war?"

The woman smiled at me and I could see enormous kindness tinged with pity. "Don't worry," she whispered, "the wounded always forget about the war just before they..."

"Good morning, Sandy!" Doctor Rheis greeted cheerfully.

The woman left before I could introduce her.

4

Propped up by pillows, I sat facing a wall of bright windows. I wondered why they put me here, in this lonely empty room painted yellow with its slick tile floor and its disappearing ceiling. It reminded me of another place, different but similar. There were no windows in this other place, yet if I never had another memory, I'd remember the curtains.

"Ah, here's our Sandy enjoying our bright and happy sun room," Doctor Rheis's voice echoed. I struggled to look around, but discovered the nurses had a surprise for me. I was secured to the chair. I could hardly move.

"Look at you!" he practically sang as he walked into my sight range. "You're tracking sounds. That's a very good sign."

"I want to get out of here," I growled, "but I can't because they tied me up. You untie me, okay?"

"Well, well," he said, "you're getting beyond the nonsense syllables and using a couple of real words. Now, whether they are the words you want to use...well, that'll be up to the speech therapist to find out. I've put an order on your chart to get you started this afternoon."

What was it with these people? I could hear myself. Every word I said was exactly what I wanted to say. Either they weren't really trying to understand me, or they were pretending I was crazy. I wasn't crazy. The woman in the pinafore understood me. She said so. Where was this woman? She was supposed to be looking for Penny. These people had taken my sister and hidden her. Maybe they were the crazy ones. That was it. These people were nutbuckets.

"Your motor reflexes are improving," Doctor Rheis winked, "but that doesn't mean you're ready to be hobbling around the corridors. The night shift tells me you've taken to midnight wanderings. Your right leg is too weak and unstable for stunts like that. I've put an order on your chart for the nurses to keep restraints on you at all times. You'll fall and hurt yourself, and I doubt your skull will take much more in the way of abuse. Do you understand?"

I tried to nod my head, let him know I was listening. He began to laugh.

"What's this? Are you sticking your tongue out at me?"

No, I wasn't. I was nodding my head.

He winked again, "Tell you what, I'll go away and let you rest up for your afternoon therapy."

"You are a fruitcake," I said. Then I laughed because I knew he couldn't understand.

When he was gone I tugged at the ropes and bands, stretched them until the knots were in my hand. With nimble fingers I worked to make them loose, then I slid down in the chair, found myself sitting free upon the floor. Getting up was a chore. My right arm dangled useless and my right leg was too heavy with sleep to be much help. Using the chair as a prop, I wriggled myself upright, then leaned against it wondering what next.

"You ain't gettin' far like that."

I raised my eye to glance about. I'd never seen him before. His face was almost lost to his beard but I could tell he was young, probably early twenties. He wore a grey jacket and grey slacks with a stripe at the side. A funny little cap nested in the thick red curls of his hair and a sword hung from his belt.

"I've seen 'em busted up worse'n you afore, but they was usually dead."

While I stared at him, it occurred how clearly I could see him, like the woman in the pinafore. "You got a name?" I asked.

"Ben O'Riley is me."

"You talk funny."

"So do you."

"You're dressed funny, too," I added.

He smiled while he studied me, as if he thought I didn't have room to talk. I had no idea what the nurses dressed me in these days and wondered if I should be humiliated. For a moment I was aware my right eye was trying to peek through a thick mucus film. I started to rub the socket with my fist, but the pain was almost unbearable.

"My face hurts," I said.

He shook his head, "Be right surprisin' if it didn't, the way it looks."

"What do you mean?"

"My momma brought me 'n my brothers up to be p'lite. She always told us, 'If you can't say somethin' nice, you best keep your mouth shut.'"

His remark sounded like an insult, and I tried to think up a smart reply, but the exercise made me dizzy. I decided to sit down, but my body didn't wait for the chair. My backside slapped the tile while my left arm groped the air.

"You might wanna take it easy," Ben O'Riley said before he turned and left me alone.

My head was pounding with pain and my butt was bruised. Rather than waste time worrying, I curled up on the floor and took a nap.

Sometime later my nap was disturbed by two hefty nurses who lifted me unceremoniously back into the dreadful chair and tied me there.

Prisoner at the stake. Set me on fire and let me go up in flames so I can be rid of this nightmare.

Not a chance. In marched a rotund little woman in a blue frilly dress. "My name is Mrs. Peach," she announced. "I am your speech therapist."

"You look like an over-ripe peach," I said.

"That's a good start," she chirped. "I can make out a couple of words. What we have to do is..."

I let her ramble on while I removed myself mentally to wait her out. Patience I didn't have, but I had nowhere to go, and not much else to do. I began to hum a tune.

That's when I heard the drums. They were distant at first, but the tap-tap-tapping grew louder and I knew they would be visible from the oversized windows. I struggled with the ropes and Mrs. Peach and made my way to the window sill where I collapsed with my face pressed against the glass. My eye searched the area outside looking for the drummers. Within seconds they appeared at the edge of a wooded road. Two young boys dressed in blue marched and beat their instruments. They were followed by an endless procession of men who wore similar suits of blue and carried swords and rifles. Now and again a few men passed on horseback, but mostly they went on foot.

There were so many. I tried to wave at them with my left hand. "Help!" I screamed. If I could just get their attention, I figured they'd rescue me and assist in finding Penny. "Oh, please!" I begged, beating the glass with my fist. Tears streamed from my left eye and stung my tender, swollen flesh, rubbed salt in my wounds.

The same hefty nurses were at my side, lifting me up and carrying me out of the Sun Room, back to my bed.

"After that little demonstration you won't get any speech therapy today," one of them said, like I was going to miss it.

They strapped me tight to the bed and covered me with blankets, not bothering to ask if I wanted to be buried beneath covers on a warm day. When they were gone someone began to whimper. So pathetic, I thought. The whimpers grew louder until they surrounded me and entered my head, made me so dizzy I thought my brain would explode.

So tired. I was so very tired.

A peaceful quiet stalked my room, crept up like heavy fog waltzing in on cat's feet.

"You think she should go back to intensive care?" a nurse asked.

"Intensive care's expensive," Doctor Rheis said. "Her parents don't have insurance. I told them she probably won't live a year like this, with or without hospitalization. They want to take her home. With all that fluid on her brain, it's surprising that child can think at all. And...she is dying. If I were dying, I'd want to die at home. Wouldn't you?"

5

I was in a covered wagon, a bumping, rolling thing that had no mercy, cared nothing about the pain inside my head.

Persecution and torture, that's what this was.

"I want to stop moving," I complained.

The wagon rolled along oblivious to my discomfort.

"My dad won't like this," I asserted. "He'll tell a bunch of his cousins about this and they'll want to know what's going on, and I'll tell them to burn this stupid wagon."

No sympathy came. I had to be more forceful.

"I am going to barf!" I yelled.

The wagon pulled to a rough halt.

"What's wrong Sandy?"

I knew that voice.

"Sandy? What's the matter? Are you sick."

Why couldn't I see? Where was my peep hole? I reached to my face and felt the bandages taped to my eyes. This won't do, I thought, trying to tear the gauze off.

"Sandy..."

"Dad? That's my dad. I hear my dad. Dad!"

"Sandy, calm down. I'm right here."

"Dad," I whispered, "Somebody kidnapped me. They threw me in a covered wagon and made me ride in it so they could jolt my head and make me suffer..."

"I don't understand you. The doc said you've got brain damage. I'm not sure what that means...but it makes it hard to understand you."

"No, Dad, I still have my brain. They didn't want that...but...wait...they kidnapped Penny. Penny? Where's Penny? Help! Please! Oh, I don't like this!"

Somebody was shaking me, telling me to settle down and behave. I knew it must be the kidnappers who forced me to ride in the covered wagon. I poked my fingers into my ears to keep my brains from spilling. All that shaking generated more pain than a person should have to live through.

"I'm really hurting," I cried.

The kidnapper wasn't shaking me anymore.

The covered wagon started moving again, but this time more slowly. The bumping wasn't quite as horrible.

"It's nap time," I said, curling myself into the corner of the wagon, waiting for the ride to be over.

I wasn't in the wagon anymore. This place was quiet, and the smells were familiar, especially the chicken and dumplings. My mother's cooking dinner, I thought.

Why didn't I think of that before? I was home in my room, taking a nap on my bed, and Mother was making dinner. Dad was probably out on the road somewhere, hauling new cars from Michigan to Memphis, or Corinth, or Tupelo. Penny was most likely out working in the fields, or maybe she was up at the barn feeding the horses. I should be helping her.

I wasn't very good at helping Penny with chores; I was mostly good at helping her get into trouble. Wait. It was coming back to me. I was helping. I could remember we went to the barn and the grain bin was empty. Dad said we could take Mom's car into Jackson and buy a hundred pounds of grain. I'm sure that's what we did because it was in my memory.

Penny was driving. No, I was driving. Who was driving?

Stop. Freeze the frame to hold the picture steady.

Penny was driving. We were leaving Jackson taking the short-cut home through Henderson past Chickasaw State Park.

"Let's stop at the park," I suggested.

"We've got to feed the horses," she said, "We don't have time."

"Okay," I said. That's what I said.

Okay. Easy as that.

Okay. It was an easy thing to say. Penny kept driving, we were going home.

Taking the hundred pounds of grain.

To feed the horses.

We loved our horses, Penny and me.

Penny was my sister, my best friend...

My mind was turning slowly, allowing the incident to play again, play again, play again...

Stuck frame. Stuck picture in my mind.

My memory was working.

"See?" I said, hoping Dad would hear and that he would know I still had my brain because my mind was in there, spitting out these pictures.

Pictures began to move.

Big hill up ahead. We started up the hill. A blue car. Green car. Blue? Freeze the frame. Check it out. Yes, a blue car. It's in the way, not moving. Big gravel truck coming down the road, aiming for us. I can see it when I make the picture stop.

It's moving again. Penny hits the brakes. We can't stop. We're skidding across the highway into a ditch.

Penny's face is bloody, but she's trying to start the car. The engine whines. It won't cooperate.

I glance out my window. The gravel truck is closing in.

"Jump out of the car!"

It's my voice, screaming.

Penny wants to start the car.

I'm not going down with the ship. Penny has all the courage. I'd rather save myself.

I start to jump out, but the truck is too close.

Loud noises, two box cars coming together. Must be a train wreck, must be.

Busting glass. Shrieking metal.

I'm on the ground unable to see what's happening.

"You've been hit," he said, kneeling over me. I felt saturated with so much sickness that I would never get over this feeling. My eyes were sticky warm with blood, and my head was pounding out of control.

"Must have been a glancing blow," he said, holding my head off the hard pavement. I could make out his face and saw that he was about my age, and that he wore the uniform of the grey side.

"The fighting is all around us," he said. "I can't tell which way is which. Guess that hardly matters 'cause we're all gonna die before we get to Nashville."

An explosive cracking sound rang out and a flash shot past my eyes. He fell beside me, and I knew he was dead before his body touched the ground. His chest gaped wide as if he'd run into a chain saw. I couldn't tell what was him and what was me. Our blood was spilling freely, staining the earth all around.

A horseman rode close, pausing to examine the

mess below. I stared up at the belly of his horse, was reminded why we went to Jackson. "Penny," I called out, "Penny! We have to go home."

"Try to be still," a woman said. "We're getting ready to put you in the ambulance."

"Penny was driving," I said.

The woman stood and called out, "I think this one's trying to say there was someone with her."

"Over here!" a man yelled. "This one went through the windshield!"

"Somebody shot the boy," I said.

"You're in shock," the woman soothed. "Just keep still."

They shoved me in the ambulance, said they'd call another for Penny. I made a fuss they couldn't ignore and they decided to keep us together.

I remember reaching out to my sister while she lay so quietly beside me. It was a painful ride.

A bumping rolling thing, that ambulance, or maybe it was a covered wagon.

"Make the pictures go away," I pleaded, pulling at the bandages wrapped across my eyes.

6

When I awoke it seemed someone had glued my eyes shut; there was no light, but I knew I'd been away for awhile. Days were missing, days stolen by a thief who took advantage of my confusion. I had been guilty of crimes; never crimes this cruel.

"Did we feed the horses yet?"

Someone was brushing my hair, separating it into three long strands to braid. I hated braids. Penny liked braids.

When the unwanted design was fixed in place, a brief reprieve ensued. My date book wasn't jammed full of interesting activities, so I waited for the next insult.

Not long to wait. A hand touched a washcloth to my face, gently patted my forehead, forgot gentle, began tearing away my flesh.

"Stop! Stop it!"

"Sandy. Quit that. Let go. What did I say? Now, let go."

...Mom?...

"That's a good girl. Keep your hands down. I'm going to pull the tape now—it might hurt."

"You're ripping off my face!"

"Just a few more pieces."

I sat on my hands, endured.

"There you are," Mom said. "Your eyes look puffy, but I think you could open them, if you'd try. C'mon. Let's see your peepers."

My what? Peepers was a baby word. I resented being treated this way, talked to as if I were an infant. "Mom!" "Well, well, you're getting a few regular words back in your vocabulary. Aha! I see some eyes behind those yellow and purple bruises. The doctor wants you to try focusing on things close to you for a few days. Don't strain, or you'll get a headache." Get a headache? Get real. My head was already one huge misery and my right arm and leg were contributing to growing feelings of hostility. They felt heavy, disconnected to their control center, disconnected to me. I scooted myself to the edge of the bed and tried to stand. Mother was immediately at my side, being motherly, making sure I didn't fall.

First steps are always dangerous.

For an infant.

"Move!" I commanded my right foot. It didn't exactly jump to obey. Instead, it dragged across the floor. I pushed toward the doorway leading to the hall. My right arm dangled, but it wasn't limp and useless, it was a coward refusing to be abused further. Once I was out in the hallway I trudged along, my left foot out front pulling the load.

Memory is strangely selective. Suddenly I was remembering how Penny would get me out of my crib when I was one and she two. It was usually midnight, both parents were asleep, and she would be wide awake, ready to get on with her life, and mine. "Let's go rock-a-by," she'd say, and I'd sleepily obey, tripping along behind while she led us into the living room, straight to the big rocking chair in front of the heat stove. There we'd sit, side by side, rocking, rocking, rocking.

Like a stuck frame. Pictures coming back. Curtains.

"Mom!"

"I'm right here."

"Where's Penny?"

Through swells of bloated tissue and film across my lenses, I could see Mom's face. She suddenly resembled shattered porcelain and left me standing unattended, alone and frail. I couldn't see more than a few feet and I didn't know where she went. I maneuvered slowly, turning back in the direction of my room. On the way I noticed a full length mirror on the wall. A bent skeletal creature with a stretched distorted head stared back at me with repulsive eyes. It was a shock. I'd never seen anything so horrible in appearance. Not polite to stare. I looked away as subtly as possible and took myself back to bed.

Curling into my soft feather mattress, I tried to spot the prancing, dancing cat I knew lurked in the shadows and prepared to pounce.

"Sandra."

Only one person could call me that and live.

"Penelope!" I emphasized every syllable. She liked her name as much as I liked mine. "Well! Aren't you a fine traitor!"

"What do you mean?" she asked, taking a seat at the edge of my bed. I grabbed her braid and gave it a tug. "Ouch!"

"I've been through Hell trying to find you! Where've you been?"

"Right here," she said. "Good grief, Sandra, you look awful! What made you wanna go and lose so much weight? You look like a scarecrow!"

She stood and stepped back to get a better view. "You need some food, that's what you need."

"You think so?"

"Oh, definitely. Like this you could stand under a clothesline in the rain and not get wet."

"You think so?"

"Most assuredly. I'm going to fix you a snack." I settled back and breathed easily. I had to get busy, regain my strength.

She returned shortly with a sandwich, a glass of milk, and a plate of chocolate chip cookies. I sat up and sniffed the sandwich suspiciously, parted the bread and inspected the middle. "Liverwurst! I hate liverwurst. You, of all people, know how much I hate this stuff."

"It's good protein, and has iron to build up your blood. Eat it.".

It did not help to argue with she-who-issued-orders. Though kind-hearted and well-meaning, she was bossy from the get-go. I took a bite and nearly puked. Penny raised an eyebrow disapprovingly. "Can I at least take the crust off?" I asked.

She nodded. "Not much food value in bread crust."

"Thanks."

When the nutritious horror was finished, I happily devoured the cookies and milk.

"Now," she said, "we're going to the potty so you can empty yourself."

When we were toddlers, Penny was terribly ashamed of me. At the age of eighteen months I still messed in my pants. Penny potty trained herself when she was eleven months. Mother couldn't train me. An incorrigible brat, that was me. Penny figured me out, knew I enjoyed attention, and set about giving me plenty. Every time my accidents occurred, she pulled my elastic pants open from the back and said loudly,

"Sandy is making stinkies!" This didn't bother me in the beginning, because we were usually at home, but Penny understood consistency. During nursery school, at the market, the babysitter's, even in the living rooms of our many relatives, she'd declare, "Sandy is making stinkies!"

I didn't feel a need to empty myself, but my memories were very clear...and Penny was consistent. "Good idea," I agreed.

Mother's footsteps were outside the bathroom. I didn't think to tell her where I was, being more interested in this immediate project, which I'd been working on for at least thirty minutes.

"Sandy? Sandy? Where are you?"

On the throne, I thought. Mom heard my thinking and pushed the door open. "How'd you...? Never mind. Now, aren't you clever. That doctor said you'd stay incontinent until.... Well, you aren't incontinent, are you?"

I tilted my head carefully and squinted up at her.

"You need some help getting back to bed?"

"Penny wants me to sit here until I'm thoroughly empty."

Mom was silent for a few seconds, then she said, "I understand some of what you're saying. Try to say it again."

"Penny put me here. I have to wait until she tells me I'm finished."

"Okay, I know the words are there—I can make out a few of them. You're speaking too quickly. Try again, slowly."

"I - am - taking - a - dump."

"There you go!" Mom sounded uncharacteristically enthusiastic about my project.

"Penny - put - me - here."

Mom grew quiet again, then remarked in a slow monotone, "Penny put you there?"

I nodded.

She shook her head, asked again, "Penny put you there?"

I nodded.

"You need help getting back to bed?"

"Okay," I said. My legs were numb from sitting so long, and I was tired of waiting for Penny to come back for me.

7

The fighting was getting out of hand outside my room. All that screaming and shooting and dust, how was I supposed to sleep? I dragged across the floor, cranked the handle and closed the window.

I guess I didn't crank fast enough. Three of the blue soldiers sneaked in and were crouching in the corner, holding their rifles, looking scared and cowardly. I dragged over and dropped down beside them.

They stared at me, and I at them, and we spent about an hour like that, not getting to know each other. Eventually the youngest boy—he couldn't have been fifteen—said, "We are twice outnumbered in this skirmish."

One of the others interrupted, "We were hoping we could surrender."

"Oh no," I said. "I'd never surrender. Go down fighting, that's what I'd do."

Who gave up the ship? bailed out? left Penny alone at the helm? On second thought I asked, "Who would you surrender to?"

"General Johnston."

"Is he a pretty good Joe?" I asked.

"Albert Sydney Johnston."

"Well, then, is he a pretty good Al?"

They exchanged unknowing looks and I could tell they didn't know Albert Sydney enough to hazard a guess. "Maybe you could make a run for it," I suggested.

"There's no place to..." the youngest started, but his voice cracked and he dropped his chin to his knees and sobbed. I wasn't very skillful handling other people's emotions so I focused on my feet, recalled a popular Linda Rondstadt tune, and began to hum. Until I noted the problem.

"Hey! What's going on! There's something wrong here," I protested, observing that my right ankle was puffed fat with swollen flesh while freshly healed scars crisscrossed like railroad tracks up and down the side of my leg. The boys in blue stretched to look.

"Could be a lot worse," one said.

"Yeah," another added, "you coulda lost the whole leg."

The youngest ceased his sobs and nodded.

"I'm getting really mad about this," I said.

"About what?"

"Somebody is trying to wreck my head, and now they're breaking my bones!"

"Mostly bruises and cuts," one said. "If you got some broken bones, they're probably in your...

The young one coughed before the speaker could finish.

"In my what?"

They were studying my face when a thunderous explosion ripped the thicket of pines a few yards from my window. I lowered my head between my knees and waited for the ceiling to cave in.

"What're you doing down there?"

Looking up I met Mom's questioning gaze. She lifted me as easily as she would a rag doll from the corner and plopped me on the chair before my writing desk.

"We're hiding," I said.

Mom inhaled deeply and sighed. "I brought a pan of warm water, a washcloth, and a towel. You think you can give yourself a spongebath?"

"Mom, we're hiding."

She surveyed the room. "We? Who else is here?"

With much effort, I turned my head from side to side, realized my companions were gone. "They musta took my advice and made a run for it," I said. "What's that?"

"That's warm water for you to wash yourself. It's not gonna stay warm for long."

"I'd rather take a shower."

"You aren't ready to manage a shower."

"I'd rather take a shower."

"You want me to wash you?"

"I'm not a baby."

"Okay," she said. "Yell if you need help."

When she was gone I took hold of the washcloth with my left hand and tried to grasp the soap with my right. The soap slid across the desk and flew through the air, hitting the side of my bed and breaking into several pieces.

This would be a soapless sudsing. Dipping the face cloth in the water and squeezing out most of the moisture, I rubbed my neck, patted the tender tissue around my eyes, and washed my hands.

"All done," I said.

"Not good enough," Penny said, walking into my room and sitting across from me.

"I scrubbed my neck. Look...squeaky clean." I bent my head so she could observe this truth.

She frowned and wrinkled her nose. "You want

people to smell you before they see you? You need to wash again. Use the soap and wash everything."

"I'm too tired."

"Mom's gonna scrub you up, like she did when you were an infant."

"No she won't."

"Act like a baby, you'll get treated like one."

"Okay, okay." Indignant, I redipped the cloth, glanced up, "How about a little privacy?"

"Don't forget the soap." She kissed the top of my head and left, closing the door.

"Wait!" Too late. I'd have to get it myself. I couldn't glide gracefully over and balance while bending to pick up the soap chips, but I figured I could lower myself from chair to floor and scoot. I ended up falling, the back of my head bumping the hard wooden seat.

War is ugly. Terrorists are everywhere, adding to the confusion and multiplying the casualties.

A terrorist was in my skull trying to plant a bomb, but it detonated before it was in place. I desperately clutched at my head, covered all the openings, prevented my senses from escaping in the midst of chaos.

This was a dangerous battle I'd got myself mixed with.

Mixed with.

Mixed up.

Tricked.

Tricksters.

In my brain.

"Penny! Come back!"

Soldiers ran past me, around me, behind me. They crawled over me like I was already a dead thing.

"I'm not!" I cried.

"Sandy! Sandy, stop flailing your arms. Stop right this minute or you'll hurt yourself!"

Mom was squatting at my side.

"I'm not dead!" I whimpered.

"Of course you're not," she said. "You're alive and well and getting better everyday."

"...Mom?"

"Yes?"

"Do I have to be in this war?"

"You're just confused," she said, "and you're having a lot of pain. You know I'd take it all away if I could."

"I'm too young...and I didn't join so why should I have to keep getting shot at and tortured...and the terrorists really should leave me alone...I haven't even done my senior year. Mom, they have to let me graduate, don't they?"

"Yes," she said, "they have to let you graduate."

I was having trouble focusing, but I could see her face and her eyes were red. I didn't know what was wrong with her. My mom had never cried before, at least not that I'd witnessed. "Did you get shot, too?" I asked.

She shook her head no and pulled a crumpled handkerchief from a pocket, blew her nose.

"Can you check my back?" I asked. "See if they shot me in the back."

"Why would you think that?"

"Look at my leg." I tried to lift it so she could examine the scars, but was distracted by the washcloth near my foot on the floor. Bits and pieces came back. "Penny wants me to wash again."

Mom's eyes grew wide and I could see their red more clearly.

"I'm not a baby, you know. I can wash myself all over so people won't smell me before they see me. But I need soap. It broke. Must've been cheap soap."

Mom went away, came back with a new bar and a fresh washcloth. "I have an idea," she said, helping me stand, walking me into the bathroom.

After nearly ten minutes, Mom had me sitting in the bathtub. She placed the stopper over the drain and started the water. When it was past my knees, she shut it off.

"If I leave, will you promise to yell if you need help?"

I was already busy scrubbing my right ankle, hoping the railroad tracks would wash away.

"Sandy!"

"What?"

"I'm going to be in the kitchen. When you're finished with your bath, yell. Promise me you'll do that?"

"Okay."

She turned to go.

"...Mom?"

"Yes?"

"Tell Penny I'm washing everywhere."

8

I gradually learned to manage my bath and dress myself, though I wasn't sure what I was wearing from day to day. The mirror in my bedroom was missing, as was the hall mirror. I limped into the kitchen, plopped unceremoniously onto a chair and asked Mom about them. She merely shrugged and washed another dish.

"Must be a burglar," I said.

"What're you talking about?" Mom asked.

"The mirrors. Maybe a burglar got them."

Mom frowned at me before grabbing a bucket and starting for the door. From the way she was dressed in snake boots and a sunbonnet I knew she was heading for the garden.

"Must've been recent," I said before she got out the door. She didn't reply. When she was gone I mumbled, "Had to be recent. Wonder if I was asleep. Must've been asleep, or I would've heard."

Mom didn't seem to care that a thief had broken in and taken our mirrors. She was different and I didn't know why. My fault I imagined, because I was always such a bad seed, causing trouble, making Mom and Dad unhappy, getting Penny into trouble.

Maybe it was payback time and They were getting even with me.

Day to day Mom allowed herself to be absorbed in chores, Dad stayed away and only returned briefly once every few weeks, and Penny seemed to have moved.

Her room was empty.

This I discovered early one morning. The noise of another skirmish between the boys in blue and the boys in grey disturbed my rest and I crawled from my bed, made my way to Penny's room. Her door was shut. Penny never shut her door.

Opening it slowly, I poked my head in and searched the darkness. My eyes weren't picking up anything so I flipped on the light switch.

Her writing desk was empty and her bed looked odd. I shuffled over and lifted the spread, saw the mattress was bare beneath it. Her closet was also bare. No shoes, clothes, or even boxes on the shelf. The walls were stripped of pictures and the window was without drapes. Taking a seat on her bed, I stared into my hands and felt more like a hollow, rotten, worthless tree stump than anything else in the world.

I wasn't much help to Mom, but I meandered about the house as best I could manage and dusted furniture or folded clothes. Now I noticed a basket full of linen. Pulling it close, I began folding pillow cases, wondered if I could make money folding people's clothes. Might please Mom and Dad, my making money to help out. Might reduce some of the tension of late.

Mysterious tension. I almost touched it once or twice, knew it was close by, yet concealed. Perhaps it was lurking in a shadow, or crouched behind a...?

A curtain! It had something to do with a curtain, yet I couldn't exactly pull the picture forward in my mind so I could see it. I desperately wanted to understand and maybe try to make amends.

I tried hard to remember, tried until my head ached.

Wished I were a magician.

Magicians were tricksters, able to perform miracles, like God, like the Great Spirits.

It had something to do with Them, I was certain. I wished I could remember.

"Let's go for a walk," Penny whispered.

I turned quickly to see that she'd sneaked in and was sitting at the table on my right side. No wonder I didn't know she was there. I had trouble with the entire right side of my body, frequently forgot it was part of me at all. Mysterious, all extremely mysterious.

"Penny," I whispered.

"Yes?"

"We should be magicians."

"We are magicians," she said with such conviction I believed her. Momentarily.

"Why'd you move?" I asked, trying to mask the sorrow and despair this caused me.

"We're going for a walk," she said.

"Mom's in the garden. Do you think we should go help?"

"Put your shoes on," she said.

She steadied me while I shuffled until we made it back to my room. My shoes didn't fit and I couldn't figure it out. I felt myself nearing a panic.

"That's okay," Penny said. "You can wear your sandals. Here, I'll help." She loosened the buckles to the last hole of each strap, then fastened them around my feet. The leather was tight and bit against my skin, but I dared not complain. She-who-would-be-boss had decided we were having a hike through the forest.

"Let's take the tractor," I suggested, thinking how easily I tired these days, and how painful it was to move.

"We aren't going to take the tractor," she scolded.

"Last time we did you drove through barbed wire and punctured a tire. Cost Dad five hundred dollars."

"Then let's ride the horses."

"Mom sold them."

I stared at Penny for a few seconds before I asked, disbelieving, "What?"

"Mom sold them," she said.

"Why? They're our horses! Those are our horses! She can't sell them!"

"She did."

"How d'you know?"

"Sandy!" Mom called from the front yard.

I turned to question Penny again, but she was gone, leaving me alone. I hated all this loneliness.

Lonely.

Strange.

Repulsive.

Who was this lonely, strange, repulsive girl?

I couldn't remember. What was I doing with my sandals on?

"Sandy!" Mom's voice was closer this time.

"Have to go for a walk...the horses...not sure," I said.

"Sandy," Mom was standing in my doorway holding a small yellow kitten. "Look what I found in the garden! Where on earth do you think it came from?"

"I have to take the horses for a walk...I think...but maybe I should feed them first."

Mom clutched the tiny kitten, shook her head, and left me alone to work it out for myself.

Spinning, spinning, spinning, like silken threads on spider feet. They kissed the cloth and cloaked my brain. And I was lonely, strange, repulsive and miserable while I tried frantically to work it all out.

9

"This one is for Tuesday."

"That's right," Mom said.

"Is today Tuesday?"

"Today is Saturday."

"Why can't I have Saturday?"

"Saturday is in the wash."

"Oh."

I was remarkably agreeable, and more often than not I found myself in this amiable mood, even when I had to wear Tuesday on Saturday.

Mom plucked my Tuesday bib off the kitchen table and tied it loosely around my neck. I wore it like a messy child. Mom made one for each day of the week and she spent several afternoons carefully crafting their edges with bright embroidered flowers. Didn't need them, actually. Only wore them because Mom expended such effort and energy making them. Wore them to please her, because she seemed desperately depressed, and it was the least I could do.

The kitten Mom found in the garden and who I nicknamed Kat, liked my bibs. She'd sit in my lap at mealtime and wait for miscellaneous goodies to dribble down my chin and drop on the embroidered flowers and leaves, then she'd skillfully pick them off with her furry feline paws and sample them with her raspy tongue.

On this morning Kat was busy checking out the

oatmeal that didn't make it into my mouth. She paused to glare at me after tasting the cereal.

"Mom?"

"What is it?"

"Kat says there isn't enough milk and sugar."

"Kat said that? I didn't hear her."

"She has a very soft voice."

Mom left the dishes she was washing and retrieved the milk and sugar, added both until sweet granules floated thick in the pool of white liquid. "I think that's enough."

Mom had lost much of her usual patient nature, and I tried to be watchful, careful not to burden her when she reached her limit. It was getting shorter, her tolerance for things, and I wondered where Dad was when she obviously could use some help with her problems.

Often I wondered what they were, these problems, and I was curious if they had anything to do with the war skirmishes all around us. Had to be some way of forcing that to our advantage. Maybe I could fold clothes for the troops. I'd insist they pay me real money. Not Confederate stuff. I think I read about that kind of currency. I'd fold clothes for regular money. Or gold coins. Or maybe I'd trade them labor for one of their horses.

"I'm gonna get a job," I heard myself say.

Mom turned to flash a strange look at me, but she didn't object to the idea. Slowly her expression slipped from her face and she said with a wink, "One of these days." With that she dried her hands and walked out the back door.

I sat for a time playing with the oatmeal, but it was too sweet to finish. I leaned over to set it on the floor for Kat and suddenly found myself unbalanced. Kat, who'd been comfortably nestled in my lap, sailed through the air with the grace of a trapeze highflyer and landed firmly on four feet. I sailed with less grace onto the hard cedar floor, smashing my shoulder. Kat huffed and hissed and hopped out of sight. I lay there thinking how dangerous that chair was, and reminded myself to take a look at it later; perhaps I could fix it.

My next task was figuring out how to get up. I couldn't just lounge around waiting for Mom. Mom already had too many problems of her own.

"Penny," I called.

No answer.

"Penny!"

Still nothing.

"Penny! Can you come help me?"

The reply I hoped for wasn't to be had, and then I reminded myself that my sister couldn't possibly hear me.

She didn't live here anymore.

I knew.

Sometimes I forgot things. I didn't forget that.

Yet she occasionally returned to visit me. I knew she'd always be there for me. We were close, twin spirits, bonded buddies. Best friends.

When we were small children Penny took a sharp needle from Mother's sewing basket and pricked my finger, then she pricked her finger, and we pressed our bloody hands together sharing the fluid of our life lines.

"Now we're blood sisters," she said proudly.

I didn't mention we were already blood sisters, but I knew what she meant.

"I could use a hand," I called out now, hoping for a miracle. More time passed and I realized I had to do this alone. Rolling onto my stomach, I pulled hard, until gradually my knees were near my chest, and then I pushed with all my might until my folded legs propelled my body upward. And then I bumped the back of my head on the bottom of the kitchen table.

Grumbling and cursing under my breath so They wouldn't hear, I leaned backwards, grabbed tight on the chair that put me on the floor in the first place, and hoisted myself to a standing position.

Kat had returned and was perched lazily on the table, methodically dipping one of her front paws into Mom's coffee cup. She left her sponge-foot in the cold coffee a few seconds, then lifted it to her face and slurped.

Too much cream. That's why Kat liked Mom's coffee. I made a mental note to suggest Mom cut down on the cream.

"What's going on in here?"

"Huh?"

"What was all the commotion?" Mom asked. "I could hear you way down in the garden." Mom's eyes were busy assessing the scene.

"You put too much cream in the coffee," I said.

"Why's your oatmeal on the floor?"

"Kat wanted it."

"Sandy! Don't encourage bad habits! And what is she doing on the table!?"

"She's having some coffee."

"Get! Scat! Shoo!"

I watched Kat scamper off towards my bedroom and safety, and I felt guilty for being one of Mom's problems.

Mom dumped what was left of my breakfast in the garbage and emptied her coffee into the sink. "I'm going to town," she said. "You want to watch television while I'm gone?"

"Okay."

She tuned in a game show and positioned my chair a few feet from the set. When I was safely seated, she went to her room and changed clothes, then left out the front door.

I hated this chair. It was too low, requiring extra strength and effort to rise when I wanted up. I wanted up now, and managed, in spite of the stupid chair, to reach the window in time to see Mom back out of the car shed and drive away.

Odd. I didn't remember Mom's car looking like that. Seemed to me Mom's car was larger, and it definitely used to be a different color. Could be the work of terrorists.

Just then a familiar sound was winding its way along the narrow country road which connected our lengthy driveway to civilization. It was leaving the road—this thing belonging to the sounds I recognized—and making a beeline for the house. I remained in my chair, continued to watch television. Soap operas now. Strange characters lived on soap operas, and I was beginning to like them because I could depend on them to be there every afternoon, five days a week. That was important. Knowing someone would be there even if they were weird.

A car door opened and slammed shut in the yard outside. Two characters argued about divorce and custody rights on the soap set. Footsteps briskly crossed the porch. One of the soap characters slapped the other, and then they embraced passionately.

Someone was loudly rapping on the front door just as a commercial for diapers replaced the soap-scenario. Struggling and grumbling, I labored out of the chair.

This damned chair!

I hated this chair.

Maybe I'd burn it before Mom returned.

"Hello?" a familiar voice called through the door.

"Hello," I yelled back.

"Sandra? That you?" The voice used my formal name.

"Yeah."

"Sandra, I've got a certified letter. I see your Mom's car is missing. You want to sign for the letter?"

I thought about the voice. Very familiar.

"I can't stand out here all day."

"Okay," I said.

I stood inside the door and waited.

"Sandra, you've got to open the door."

"Okay." I turned the knob and pulled it wide, looked into our mail carrier's face. Couldn't remember her name.

"I'm sorry but the screen is locked, too," she said, holding the certified letter so I could see it.

"That's okay," I said, wondering why she thought it necessary to apologize about the screen since she hadn't locked it. I fidgeted with the locking mechanism until it gave way, and pushed the door free. She handed me a ballpoint and positioned the certified mail on a clipboard.

"Sign here," she said, pointing to a line, "and then sign here," she indicated a green slip of paper on the envelope.

My vision was often blurred, but I wasn't seeing more than one of things these days, except when I was tired. I bent my head in close to the places where I was to sign.

"Sandra, dear," she said, "do you think you can manage?"

"Huh?"

"I'm sorry...I hadn't realized. Do you think you can write?"

I brought the ballpoint up to my face, studied it, and couldn't remember what to do with it.

"I, ah, why don't you just make an 'X'?"

The motion came automatically, and I saw my hand guide the pen to the papers and make a mark. Not really an 'X', just a mark. The carrier smiled and handed me the certified letter, along with several more.

"What's this?" I asked.

"That's the rest of your mail."

"My mail?"

"Yes. One is addressed to you. The others are for your mom and dad."

"Oh."

"Well, I've got a route to deliver. Better be on my way."

"Okay."

"You gonna be alright?"

"Sure."

She seemed not to believe me and paused a few seconds. Then she shrugged and left. I pulled the screen shut, allowed the door to stay open, and carried the mail to the kitchen table. I sorted it, had trouble reading the words, but recognized the one with my name. After removing it from the pile, I pulled my blouse up and tucked it carefully between my waistband and waist, then dropped my blouse to hide it.

Didn't want anyone to steal it.

Might be a secret letter.

Never could tell.
Hard to say.
During times of war.

10

First thing I wanted to do was take care of the chair. I tugged and pulled, pushed and heaved, and nearly killed myself trying to make it budge. It gave not an inch! I'd never be able to burn it before Mom got home if I couldn't get it outside.

I pondered my dilemma, considered charities. Charities took away good stuff, gave it to people in need. This was a fact I was certain of, since it's how we acquired some of our better possessions. Not that we were in need of hand-outs, but we did live a step or two above poverty some years, and a long stride below it others. It was during those long strides when we accepted items of good-will, as Mom called them.

I tried using the telephone book to locate a charity. I thumbed through to a random page, but couldn't quite organize my thoughts, or coordinate them with my project. I knew there was a method to what I wanted to do so I concentrated until my brain felt bruised.

Maybe if I just started dialing.

With phone in hand, I pushed buttons. Then I held the receiver to my ear and listened. At first nothing happened, but given my patience I eventually made contact.

"What number, please?" a woman's voice asked.

"Hello?"

"Yes. What number, please?"

"I don't know the number."

There was a short pause.
"How may I help you?" she asked.
"I need someone to take it away."
"I'm sorry. This is the operator. I can only put your calls through."
"Can you get a charity for me?"
"You need to dial Information."
"I don't know how."
Another short pause.
"Stay on the line," she said.
After a few rings, someone answered, "Central Baptist."
"Hello," I said, "can you come and take it away?"
"I'm sorry, can you say that again?"
"I have a chair I don't want. When I sit down, it's too low, and it makes my arms hurt when I try to get out of it. I really hate it. I'd burn it, but my head is starting to hurt, and I don't think I can get it outside."
"You mean you have a chair you'd like to donate?"
"Okay."
"Can you hold on a minute while I find our receptionist? She handles charitable donations."
I waited, then repeated my problems to the receptionist and told her where I lived. She promised to send a truck for it the next day, and she thanked me for my generosity.
I felt quite righteous and full of goodness at that moment, and wondered if They were watching. Probably not. They only looked my way when I was misbehaving.
I was beginning to wonder if Mom was ever coming home. It was getting later with each new minute. My stomach growled, reminding me I hadn't eaten

lunch, and I went to the refrigerator and peered inside. Mom had prepared a peanut butter and jelly sandwich wrapped in wax paper. I unwrapped it and ate while I leaned against the counter. Before I closed the refrigerator I saw a glass of milk had also been poured, so I drank it. Then, almost as an afterthought, I took the wax paper and the empty glass out of the refrigerator and placed them in the sink. Mom would be pleased at my helpfulness.

My hunger satisfied and my letter safe beneath my clothing, I sat at the table and examined Mom's mail. Strange I was having such difficulty understanding the words. Not all, but most, seemed to be in a foreign language. I rubbed my eyes until they ached, thinking maybe my eyes were deceiving me because they were tired. I'd had a great deal of trouble with them since the terrorists beat me, and this could be a leftover symptom. Eye confusion. Yes, that was it. My eyes were easily confused because of the beatings.

What was this? I definitely recognized the name on the certified envelope: Penelope.

Penny had a certified letter. From? I picked it up, held it within a few inches of my confused eyes. More foreign words. I could get the dictionary, look up these words, try to figure out what they meant.

The dictionary was usually in Penny's writing desk. I went to her empty room and searched the desk. It wasn't there. I found it in my own desk, which was almost too weird, because I had never kept it in my room before. Before what?

I carried the dictionary to the kitchen and plopped myself down at the table, began to search the book for words identical to those on the envelope.

This wasn't working. I knew how to use a dictionary, but things weren't making sense. I closed the book and pushed it away for a short while, allowed my brain to find a gear and get cranking.

Alphabet. Something to do with alphabet. Dictionaries were words listed in alphabetical order. Find the letter of the alphabet beginning a word and search for it in the book.

This took a long time, but it panned out. Eventually I had the first word located, then the second, third, and fourth. Something about the exercise forced my brain to sort and sift, assembling items into a fashion I could understand. By the time Mom arrived home it was early evening, the sun was low in the sky, and I knew.

"Mom!" I said, full of excitement.

Mom entered through the back door, dropped her purse on the kitchen table, and sat down heavily. "What's this?" she asked, noticing the dictionary and the small pile of mail.

"Penny got a certified letter from the University of Tennessee! She got the scholarship! She got it, Mom!"

Mom picked up the envelope, noted it was still sealed. "Why would you think that?" she asked.

"Look! See? It's from the university! Penny will be so happy! Now she can go to college like she dreamed. Penny's really smart, Mom. I knew she'd get it. She did! Oh, wow. Wait'll I tell her."

Mom slowly ran a finger nail along the envelope's edge and reached inside, removed a folded paper. She let it fall open from the top and I watched her face while she was reading. When her eyes watered I felt betrayed by my excitement.

"Didn't she get a scholarship?"

Mom nodded.

"Aren't you happy? Don't you want Penny to go away to college?"

Mom folded the letter and slipped it into her skirt pocket. I remembered my secret letter and reached under my blouse, made sure it was still tucked into my pants. All seemed pretty right with the day, yet I couldn't understand Mom's reaction. Maybe she was upset because Penny moved away, and with this scholarship, she'd have to move even farther.

"Are you hungry?" she asked suddenly.

"No."

"Well then, I'm going to my room."

Before she went, she turned off the television, which I'd forgotten. When she was gone, Kat waltzed down the hallway, hurried over to brush against my ankles, and meowed for her dinner.

Mom had a can of sardines open in the fridge. I dumped them all onto Kat's plate and watched while she gobbled them with delighted greed.

I wandered around the house following Kat and eventually opened the back door for her to exit into the night. Mom never emerged from her room, and before I retired to my room, I ate a few potato chips and a handful of raisins.

When I did retire, I took the dictionary. I still had my letter to decipher.

11

Safe in the privacy of my room, I dropped the dictionary on my desk, pulled out the letter, and spent an hour attempting to decipher oddly cryptic words. Who sent it? Why were they using words that required such effort and energy to understand? And who had gotten hold of the dictionary and scrambled it into such a mess? When I concentrated and used extreme patience, it was possible to match a few words from the letter with similar words from the dictionary. Problem was, I still couldn't figure out what they meant. Maybe they were trying to confuse the terrorists. Why were all Mom's letters in code, too? Could be terrorists were bothering her. Could be they were her problem.

My brain was trying to go on one of its fade-outs, making my thinking go all a-jumble. I thought, Sit still and breath steady. Let it pass. This fade-out.

Finally! I figured out it was my cousin Mark who sent the letter; couldn't figure why he was in Florida. Never heard him say anything about going there. Hard to imagine why he'd want to since there were alligators down in Florida. Had enough trouble keeping the terrorists away and staying out of the frequent skirmishes between the boys in blue and the boys in grey. Didn't need any alligators creeping about.

Gave me the shivers.

Too much to worry about.

My eyes puffed and swelled in their sockets while my little grey cells grew exhausted. After changing into pajamas, I crawled on top of my bedspread, curled up, and pulled down the shades.

I awoke early the next morning, bathed and dressed, and tucked Mark's letter into my waistband. I didn't want to open it until I was prepared to decode it. Might take hours. Even days. Tricky business, deciphering the alphabet.

In the kitchen I rummaged through the linen drawer where my bibs were neatly folded. By me. I always folded them after they were washed and dried.

I was getting sidetracked.

What was I doing?

Breakfast. I needed my bib, and found it folded carefully and lying on top of the stack of bibs. Sometimes I recognized the days of the week spelled out in colorful yarn, and sometimes I didn't, but I always recognized their designs. Butterflies were Sunday. After slipping my head through the bib's pre-tied straps, I poured cereal into my bowl.

Before I could eat, the Central Baptist Church truck arrived. Mom was still in bed asleep and I decided not to wake her. I'd surprise her later by showing her all the extra space in the living room.

Is that why I wanted to be rid of the thing? Seemed like there'd been another reason.

Just then two boys about my age came to the front door. They were dressed in suits, probably on their way to Sunday school for an hour of pious fraud. I remembered boys like that. Mean and sneaky, full of tricks. Always had a con up their slippery sleeve. Smiling at the teacher to get a passing grade. Smoking cigarettes between classes. Blaming me.

I remembered doing time in the principal's office.

Some boys said I set off the fire alarm. Looked like them, in their Sunday suits. Standing in the office, pinning the crime on me. I never busted the glass, never pulled the switch.

"You're a real trouble maker," the principal said. "You're going to end up doing time. A bad road for a young girl to follow."

"Wasn't me," I said.

Should have said, "It was them. Bad boys built the bad road."

I wouldn't forgive them their sins. Knew Who would. Wasn't my error in judgement, was it? Was Their error. Only thing I wanted to concern myself with was...?

Missing.

Something was missing. A thought?

They could see me through the window. What mischief now?

I opened the door, pushed the screen wide and looked at them.

They didn't speak. Instead they stood there and stared rudely. I glared back until the taller one cleared his throat and asked, "Y'all the people with a chair?"

"Do I look like y'all people?" I said. "Must be something wrong with your eyes. Maybe you got brain damage."

"Uh..."

I noticed cereal stuck to my bib and tried to pick it off.

"Where is it?" one asked.

"Where's what?"

"The chair."

"Oh." I stepped aside and pointed across the

room. They leaned in, then looked at me as if they weren't sure what to do next. Weren't sure what I might do, either.

"You wanna stay 'til supper, or you gonna take that away?" I was surprised to hear myself sounding like myself. They cautiously crossed the threshold, picked up the thing, and hauled it out.

"I thought she was the one killed in that car wreck," the short one whispered as they made their exit.

"Nah. It was the nice one got killed," the tall one said while throwing a smart-ass look over his shoulder. "But by the looks of her, she ain't long for."

What a couple of class-act jerks, making up crude lies. I pushed the door shut and didn't bother to watch them drive away.

Mom still hadn't gotten out of bed. I shuffled as quietly as I could manage down the hall and cracked her door. She was snoring softly, deep in sleep or dreams. Maybe I could fix a pot of coffee. She'd enjoy waking to fresh-brewed coffee.

Back in the kitchen I removed a pound of coffee from the refrigerator and pried off the plastic lid. Yet, try as hard as I could, I didn't know what to do next.

I'd made hundreds of pots of coffee. This was no different. I examined the drip machine to see if something had changed. Nope. It was the same. I checked the brand of coffee to see if Mom had switched. Same old brand. I felt myself getting angry.

The terrorists were at it again!

In my brain, moving things around, hiding information, substituting confusion!

Enough! I grabbed my head and pressed tight, let the terrorists know I knew. Knew they were in there.

A noise distracted me.

Kat was yowling and scratching at the back door. I hurried to let her in before she woke Mom. She prissed and pranced around the floor to let me know she'd had a successful night of hunting. She rubbed past my ankles once or twice, then dashed for her bowl of dry kibbles and scarfed a few down the hatch.

I took a load off, propped my elbows on the table, and wondered if I should tell Penny about the alphabet code.

No. Penny had her scholarship and soon she'd be off to Knoxville. I'd keep this cryptography project to myself. Maybe I'd even take up waiting at the mail box for the post carrier so I could decipher all the letters before Mom got them. That would be really helpful. Save Mom a lot of headaches.

I hated headaches.

Never had them before.

Wished I could remember when they began.

"Why'd you put all this stuff on the counter?" Mom asked while she tied the belt around her bathrobe.

I didn't know what she was talking about.

"Sandy."

"Huh?"

"Coffee grind and filters, a bottle of vanilla, a cup of flour, chocolate chips. What are you up to?"

"Oh. I was going to make coffee."

"With vanilla, flour, and chocolate chips?"

I looked curiously at Mom, wasn't sure what she was asking.

"Never mind," she said, putting some of the items away and preparing her own pot of coffee.

Kat sneaked under the table and crawled up my leg, nestled down in my lap, commenced to purring.

When Mom's coffee was ready, she poured a cup, added sugar and cream, which would please Kat, and carried it into the living room.

"Sandy! Come in here! Right now!"

I set Kat on the floor and hoisted myself up, followed Mom's commanding tone. She was standing in the vacant spot which once housed it. The thing. The chair.

"Where is it?"

"Gone."

"I see that. What'd you do with it?"

"The operator got rid of it."

"What operator?"

"On the telephone."

"That's ridiculous. What did you do with it?"

Too much excitement set me off, spun me in, secured me in a prison where all thinking took a holiday. I couldn't remember why the creepy church boys took the chair, but I knew it had something to do with the operator. She started it, and it was her fault now that Mom was angry.

Collapsing in a heap on the floor I began to whimper.

"Now that's enough of that," Mom scolded.

"I want my head back. This isn't my head and these aren't my eyes and this brain belongs to an idiot. I want my head, Mom. I want my head. I liked it fine. I don't like this thing, either," I tugged and pulled until the bib was off.

"Sandy, please!" Mom shouted, her tone full of anger and frustration.

I tried to stop but it wasn't me making so much fuss. Mom grasped my shoulders and helped me stand before ushering me off to my room.

12

Morning stretched, became afternoon, and I wallowed unrewarded—alone and without audience—in self pity. Kat was out in the hallway doing some serious shadow boxing. I called to her and she slipped her fur-paws beneath my door. I rolled on my side and watched while her fuzzy feet raked to and fro, her claws lazily flexing and extending, her little pads batting invisible objects. Occasionally I could see the tip of her velvet nose sniffing. She was such a curious snoop.

Curious.

Snoop.

Reminded me of...something I had. What was it?

Had to train this head to work if it was going to live upon my shoulders. Forgetfulness would not be tolerated.

Think!

Who was curious and about what?

I was.

That was it! My letter! I pulled it from my waistband, held it a few inches from my face and studied the words. It was addressed to me with a return address from Mark. For the first time I noticed the words below his name. I hurried to my desk, made myself focus on the code, until I understood: Dade County.

I tore the envelope, removed the folded paper, straightened it carefully on the table top, and dug into my desk for a notebook and pencil. I labored nearly an hour making my fingers cooperate with the pencil, making the pencil memorize the first word, copy it into the notebook: Dear.

Dear Sandy.

Ah. That was an easy line. I glanced down at the letter's body and it became a mass of mixed up scribble.

Kat, tired of being locked out, hissed and meowed until I went to the door and let her through. She jumped on the bed, yawned, arched her back to unkink her vertebrae, then snuggled into my pillow and purred a song of content.

While I watched her my thoughts tried to skip out.

Wouldn't be confused.

Stop. Refocus. Turn attention back to the desk, force self to remember the notebook.

NOW. What was I doing with the notebook?

Penny was sent off to school when she turned six. I wanted to go, didn't know what to do without her, tried often to follow her down to the bus stop. Half a dozen times I climbed up the bus steps behind her, only to be lifted and carried off again by the driver.

"I'm six, too," I would inform the driver, holding up five fingers. Five was my age at the time, and it was as far as I could count.

"We'll catch you next year," the driver would smile and wink, grabbing the handle to pull the doors shut in my face. I'd sit in the dirt and stare until the huge yellow bus was out of sight, and then I'd cry until my stomach hurt. Eventually Mom would walk down our long driveway to pick up the free local newspaper, and she'd stand quietly nearby waiting until I was ready, then we'd walk slowly back to the house together.

There I'd wait for each minute to make an hour,

frequently asking Mom if it was three-fifteen. The bus always brought my sister home at three fifteen. I'd race from the door, tearing up the gravel with my flying feet, and we'd smash into each other somewhere along the driveway.

Although Penny didn't care much for school, she enjoyed all the paraphernalia that went into her satchel: books, glue, scissors, paper, pencils, a pencil sharpener, an eraser, crayons, and her alphabet sheets. All these items she happily shared with me, yet it was the alphabet sheets I remembered now.

What about the alphabet sheets?

"I'm gonna teach these to you," Penny announced, pulling a handful of papers from her shoulder satchel one afternoon while we skipped back to the house. I took one of them from her and studied it.

"You got it upside down," she giggled.

I turned it over. She pointed her finger to one of the symbols.

"This one says Aeee. You say it."

"Aayee."

"Nope. Aeee. Try again."

"Aeee."

"Good. Now this one. It says Beee. Say Beee."

"Buzz-buzz-buzz."

"No, no. It's not a honey bee, you silly goose. Say Beee!"

"Beee!"

"Very good. I'll let you color a picture."

"I wanna pick my own," I said.

"Okay," she said, holding her satchel wide and allowing me to check out her assortment of coloring pages.

"This one," I said, grabbing a picture of three

puppies.

"That's my favorite."

"I want this one."

"Okay, wait," she said, a gleam in her eyes. "You can have it if you remember what this is." She pointed to the first symbol.

"Aeee."

"Good."

My hand went for the puppies.

"Nope. One more. What was this?"

"Beee."

"Okay," she said reluctantly. I secured the puppies and ran into the house before she could change her mind.

As first grade progressed and Penny learned the alphabet, she also learned to read. These skills she shared, using the alphabet sheets.

The alphabet sheets should be helpful now. But were they still around after all these years?

I abandoned my letter and left my room in search of...I wasn't sure. Had to be something one would keep old papers in, like a box, or a drawer, maybe even a suitcase.

I was feeling unusually perceptive.

"Oh please," I begged, "let these grey cells work."

"Who're you talking to?" Mom called from the kitchen.

"Thought one of Them might be watching. Fat chance."

"Them?"

"You know," I said, emerging from the hallway.

"Hmmm. Well, you haven't had lunch," Mom said as I passed her on my way to the basement.

"Too busy," I said.

Mom shook her head and sighed. She was stirring something on the stove and it smelled delicious, but I didn't want to get sidetracked and lose my perceptive edge while the grey cells were cooperating.

I was beginning to understand.

It was right there, on the edge of a thought.

Had to find the alphabet sheets.

"Where are you off to?" Mom asked.

"The basement."

"You can't go down there!"

I paused and glanced back. "Why?"

"You'll fall down the stairs!"

"I never fell down stairs before."

"Well, that was before, wasn't it?"

"Before what?"

"What's in the basement?"

"Penny's alphabet sheets. Remember? She always brought her lessons home for me."

"You remember that?"

"Sure."

Mom got that funny look on her face again. "What in the world do you want with them?"

"If I have the alphabet sheets I can understand the code. You know where they are?"

Mom took a hand towel off the counter and wiped her fingers. She didn't answer.

I attempted to shrug, but effected only a warped rendition of the posture. Turning around, I resumed my course towards the stairwell behind the utility room. I had to do this now while my thinking was fluid. Had to hurry.

To the basement.

Pieces of nothing crept into my mind.

Starting to erase. Screen erasing.

Had a project; it was such a good idea. Had to find the alphabet sheets before the screen went blank. Heard Mom's footsteps following and I figured she knew where Penny's stuff was stored. Had to hurry, while I could think. Wished I had some cotton. Would cram it tight into my ears' orifices. Would keep my fluid thought fluid. If I had some cotton. Terrorists lay in wait deep in the dark recesses of the stairwell. I could smell the mold and mildew of their rancid breath moments before they squeezed their clammy presence against my flesh, working their way through my thoughts, penetrating all perceptive edges, forcing me to hurry faster, faster, faster!

Mom called loudly, "Wait up!"

Startled me. Scared them away.

The steps proved to be every bit as dangerous as Mom warned, and she had to assist me by standing on the lower levels and helping me descend one at a time. When we were halfway she instructed me to hold tight on the rail while she went down and flipped the light switch, illuminating our destination.

13

Mom climbed the ladder, hoisting boxes and crates from dusty shelves. I was extremely helpful and held the ladder steady. When the basement floor was cluttered and the shelves were empty, we both sat on the cool concrete and searched for Penny's alphabet sheets. I was pleasantly proud Mom was taking such interest in this recent project since she'd made it clear she hadn't appreciated my last project.

Something about the empty space in the living room.

A mystery.

Couldn't remember.

Better to leave it.

Mom too angry.

All gone.

Screen already blank.

"Look," Mom said, holding Penny's red plaid satchel.

"Wow!" Memories marched across the battle-field of my young life, clear and colorful, tangible and touchable. I stretched my arms out to embrace my sister as she ran toward me, her black braids flying in the wind. She was six, I was five, and I was full of curiosity about what she carried in her satchel.

"I've got cinnamon lollipops!" Penny squealed with excitement.

"Oh! Didja get 'em at school?"

"A kid on the bus gave them to me," she bragged,

reaching into her satchel and pulling them out, handing one to me.

"Why?" I asked.

"I kept a secret."

"Tell me!" I said, unwrapping the lollipop and sampling a corner with the tip of my tongue.

"It was a bigger kid. She threw a book at another kid and the bus driver stopped the bus! She said, 'Who threw that book?' and the big girl looked at me. I shook my head, like I didn't know. Then the big kid gave me these!"

"Oh," I said, slurping my candy, "This is the best lolli I ever ate!"

"Yeah," she agreed, popping hers into her mouth.

"Cinnamon lollipops should taste like cinnamon," I said.

"Yes," Mom said, "They should."

"Something fell."

"Nothing fell," Mom said.

"Lollipop is gone. Can't find it. Must've fell."

"You didn't have a lollipop," Mom said.

"It wasn't me who lied to the bus driver."

"What're you talking about?" Mom asked. I could see her sitting across from me clutching the satchel.

"Once," I said, "Once Penny told a lie, conspired with a criminal—had nothing to do with me."

Mom looked surprised.

"Really," I said, brushing the floor with my fingers, searching for the cinnamon sweet.

"Everyone tells lies at one time or another," she said. "Even our Penny."

I felt suddenly guilty, like a snitch. "Don't tell her I told you that," I begged.

"Okay."

"Please, Mom. Promise you won't tell her."

"I promise."

"What are we looking for?" I asked. My mind was a blank. I hated this emptiness. It tricked me, trapped me, teased me.

Tricksters? Terrorists? Maybe they were back. Or maybe it was just a bad brain. Wasn't mine, after all. Belonged to someone else. Had to train this one.

"Penny's alphabet sheets," Mom said, opening the satchel and digging through it. "They aren't here."

Why was Mom hunting down Penny's alphabet sheets? Mom grabbed another box and sifted through its contents. I told myself I should be doing something, too, but I was feeling strange and fires were beginning to singe the fissures that separated my grey cells.

"I'm dizzy."

"Just sit still," Mom said, "and it'll pass."

I tried to sit still. The dizziness spread from head to stomach, making me nauseated. Mom was busy with the boxes and continued to talk, but her words bounced around and got jumbled in the process. Someone was trying to douse the burning fissures with water. So much water. More than I needed. I cupped my palms over my orbits to keep my eyeballs from popping out. All that pressure could burst my pipes.

I tried to say, "I'm drowning."

"I found them!" Mom exclaimed, waving a handful of papers before my face. I tried to reach for them.

"Sandy? Sandy, what's going on?"

"How long has she been unconscious?"

"Two hours." That was Mom's voice. Who was unconscious?

"We've got to admit her."

Familiar voice. Who was talking to Mom?

"I can't pay. I don't know what to do about this. There isn't any insurance, you know. Is she going to live?"

"Fluid's been accumulating. If we don't drain it she's not going to live long. She must've had a lot of pain. Has she been vomiting or complaining?"

"She does vomit, but she doesn't complain. Look, I can't pay for more..."

"I'm a physician! I can't leave her like this."

Hi, Doc! That's you. I can hear you, Doctor Rheis. See? I remember you.

"Do what you can for her, but I can't promise you'll be paid."

"This isn't the time to worry about that." Doctor Rheis sounded impatient.

I thought, I'm not worried. Penny got her scholarship. She's going to the University of Tennessee at Knoxville. Me and Mom will stay home and take care of Kat. I fold clothes. Don't know where Dad is. He doesn't come home anymore. Mom said he decided he didn't need us. That's okay. Penny got her scholarship. I think we forgot to feed the horses. I'll remind Penny.

"Hello! Did I detect some eye movement there? I think I did. Can you hear me?"

Without straining my eyes I peeked through my lashes. "Blanche," I said.

"How in the world did you remember my name?" The night nurse asked. "And look how nice you're talking! You weren't doing any real talking last time you were here."

"Where's the other lady, the old one with the bloody apron?"

Blanche wrinkled her brow and shook her head.

"Don't know who that would be. Could be you're remembering one of the surgical nurses."

"Could be. Where's my sister?"

"Are you thirsty?" She was trying to change the subject. "I'll bring you some juice."

"Penny was here with me. This is where they took her away. You bring her to see me. Tell her I'm awake now."

"I'm going to bring you some orange juice. That sound good?"

"You go get my sister."

"I think I'll go call your doctor."

I waited for more than an hour before Doctor Rheis arrived. He entered my room with the same brisk stride so familiar from that other time. "Heard you're giving the nurses a hard time?" he said.

"No—I'm not."

"Tell you what. I'm going to phone your mother and tell her she can take you home."

"Good."

"How are you feeling?"

"I'm dizzy."

He chuckled and placed a hand on my forearm, gave it a squeeze. "I'm sure you are."

"Where's the room with the curtains?"

His face was curious, as if he really didn't understand me.

"I remember the curtains. Penny was in that room with me. Where is she, and where'd all this fog come from?"

"As soon as your mother gets here we'll have a nice talk. Right now I want you to lie here quietly and get some rest."

When he was gone the fog slowly cleared and I

remembered my letter from Mark—and Penny's certified letter. And then I remembered how she brought food to my room, told me I was getting too thin; and I thought about her alphabet sheets.

Later, when Mom and Doctor Rheis came into my room looking somber and serious, I told them, "Never mind. I know where Penny is. She had to go to Knoxville to get ready for school. Now, I want to go home so I can decipher my cousin's letter."

Doctor Rheis glanced at Mom and she avoided his expression.

"If it's all right with you," Mom said to Doctor Rheis, "I'd like you to discharge my daughter now."

I grabbed the side rail of my bed and pulled myself to a seated position.

"May I talk to you in the hall," he said to Mom.

Her expression turned stubborn, but she followed him out of the room. I worked on the rail until it dropped, then swung my feet off the bed's edge, planted my soles on the floor, and managed to stand. The room rocked about like a boat on the ocean and I grabbed the bed until I was steady.

A mirror hanging above the bedside table caught my attention and I inched toward it.

"Who's that?" I did not recognize the distorted ugly face staring back.

"Where am I?

"Where am I?" I repeated.

"Help!" I screamed.

Mom raced in with Doctor Rheis close on her heels. When they neared the mirror I could see their reflections. They were standing on either side of the pitiful creature.

But where was I?

14

Nurse Blanche helped me wash myself while Mom and Doctor Rheis waited in the hallway. When I was convinced no one could smell me before they saw me, I rinsed the soap off and donned a loose shirt-shift Mom had brought.

"I don't like this dress," I complained to Blanche.

"What's wrong with it?"

"It's baggy and stupid and ugly."

"Why, you look cute as a bug in it," she said.

"I don't want to look like a bug."

"Don't you worry about what you look like. You're a pretty girl, and you'll be pretty in whatever you're wearing."

"I don't want to look like a bug."

Blanche clicked her tongue, reminded me of an old hen clucking at her brood. She was combing my hair when Mother and Doctor Rheis appeared in the doorway. They were arguing about Penny, and I could tell they couldn't seem to agree on where she was. I knew so it really didn't make any difference to me whether or not they agreed.

"I want to go now," I said.

Doctor Rheis started to say something but Mom interrupted, "As soon as the wheelchair comes."

"What's the wheelchair for?"

"You get to ride in the wheelchair."

"Nope," I said, rising off the bed. Nurse Blanche

planted a heavy hand on my shoulder, sat me back down.

"You will ride in the wheelchair," Blanche said with an authoritative tone equal to her size.

"Okay."

Blanche propelled the wheelchair and I could hear Mom and Doctor Rheis walking along behind us. When we were out of the hospital and rolling down the sidewalk in the direction of Mom's car, I saw them again.

Hadn't seen them for a week or more. Thought maybe they'd reached a battleground agreement to rest; take a break; give the old bubbling-blood-and-gushing-gore routine a respite.

A small band of boys in grey hid in the cover of the trees across the parking lot while a group of blue soldiers approached from the northeast. Two of the blues rode handsome horses while the rest marched on foot.

"It's an ambush," I whispered.

"Where?" asked Blanche.

"Right there." I pointed to the row of trees in the distance. "Gonna be shooting and screaming real soon."

"Don't encourage her hallucinations," Doctor Rheis scolded Blanche.

"Duck!" I yelled, scrambling out of the wheelchair in time to avoid a catastrophe. The boys in grey had a cannon and they were firing on the blues. Bullets whizzed in every direction, narrowly missing us. I raised off the ground, witnessed the horsemen drawing swords and heading for the woods. A second cannonball flew out, caught one of them, separated him into a part that fell and a part that stayed in the saddle. The horse went wild, running and bucking, trying to dislodge the mutilated thing on its back.

"Quick," I screamed at Mom, "Catch the horse!"

Doctor Rheis rushed to lift me off the pavement. He and Blanche fastened my seatbelt, securing me in the passenger seat of Mom's car.

"I want the horse!"

"Sandra! Hush!" Mom was really upset, afraid the soldiers would see us and start shooting at the car.

"If you catch the horse," I whispered, "I'll ride him home and I promise to feed him every day. I won't forget this time. I swear."

Mom slammed my door, but I could hear the conversation.

"Why does she do this?"

"It's part of the head trauma. Hallucinations are common. Just don't let her draw you into them," Doctor Rheis said.

"What? Are you saying my daughter's crazy? Insane?"

"I explained all of this to you and your husband months ago. It's part of the injury. She's not crazy, she's ill."

"I don't understand."

"It's kind of like being lost between the world of the living and the world of the spirits," Blanche added.

Doctor Rheis stared at Blanche, "What kind of theory is that?"

"The child doesn't belong to this world anymore," Blanche said. "She's just passing time before she meets her Maker. No telling who she sees."

"Nonsense!" Doctor Rheis barked.

The three of them continued to argue, but I got stuck on the part about meeting my Makers. I was not Their favorite person. Maybe that was the problem.

Maybe They didn't want me.

What if They were making deals with the terrorists, trying to keep me distracted so I would never meet Them?

"Mom," I said, rolling down the window, "can we go?"

As we drove away from the parking lot I noticed the skirmish was over and the soldiers had gone off to fight somewhere else, but the horse was still there and the dripping bleeding thing was still hanging in the saddle.

Somebody should bury that thing.

Not me. I just wanted the horse.

"Mom," I heard myself begging, "I promise I'll take good care of that horse. Please? Can I ride it home? Please?"

Mom didn't answer.

"Mom sold our horses," Penny said.

"But they're ours," I said. "Mom?"

"What?"

"It'll probably starve."

"Who'll starve?"

"The horse."

We were several blocks from the parking lot. Mom drew a deep breath and cleared her throat. "Sandy, if you saw a horse near the hospital, it had to belong to somebody."

"He got shot."

"Who?"

"The man on the horse."

"Sandy..."

"In half, Mom. With a cannonball. War is hell."

Mom cleared her throat a second time. "You wanna stop for a sandwich?"

"Huh?"

"The nurse said you didn't eat breakfast. If you want, we'll stop for lunch."

I said "Okay," because that's what Mom wanted me to say.

15

I came home to discover Kat asleep on my bed. Mom said she stayed in my room while I was doing time in the hospital. Such loyalty pleased me and I flopped down beside her, disturbing the pattern of her deep rest. She hissed and growled in protest at the rude awakening, then stared quizzically at me as if to ask, "Just where do you think you've been?"

"Are we still buddies?" I inquired, smoothing her silky yellow coat.

"Purrrrrrrrrrr."

"Good."

"You think you'd like to watch television?" Mom asked while she helped me take my sandals and socks off. Kat perched on her haunches and spied Mom with clever green eyes.

"Why am I wearing socks?"

"To keep your feet clean."

I studied my toes, "My feet are clean."

"Thanks to your socks."

"I hate to wear socks. Looks funny."

"They don't look funny."

"I don't want to wear socks."

"We'll see."

"I don't want to wear bibs, either."

"We'll see. Now, do you want to go to the living room and watch television?"

"No." I scratched Kat's forehead.

"Suit yourself," Mom said, carrying my shoes and socks to the closet. Before she disappeared through the doorway, she said, "If you start having pain, let me know. Doctor Rheis gave me some pills. They're supposed to make the hurting go away. But you gotta tell me when you hurt, or these pills won't do any good. Can you do that?"

I nodded. Was the least I could do. Seemed nice of Doctor Rheis to give Mom pills so she wouldn't suffer when I had pain.

Hospitals caused me enormous fatigue. Didn't know what I was doing there in the first place. Maybe having a visit with the good Doc. Nurse Blanche was a nice old bird. Could be I was visiting Blanche.

I thought I was on dry land. This floor was swaying. Who put me on a boat? Hated boats and all that went with them, like being seasick and puking until I felt purple.

Grabbing the bed post, I made the motion stop just as balloons were being popped somewhere in the near distance.

People having a party. Loud.

Who? Our nearest neighbor was a quarter mile away. Not a party kind of guy, actually. The neighbor. Old farmer John, always wearing sun-bleached overalls, riding a tractor, plowing fields. I stole melons from his patch every autumn. He shot at me with a rifle. I could remember the melons, the rifle. Missed on purpose, he said.

Didn't know he was such a noisy man. I poked my fingers inside my ears to quiet the party at farmer John's place.

Somebody was crying.

Sad and crying...and shaking...all shook up...sick.

"Sandy? What's wrong? You in pain? You want a pill? Sandy?"

Rolled up, wadded up, curling into myself, I felt like a tiny infant in a crib.

Babies aren't criminals. I told Penny I was innocent when I was a baby. Got bad later. Something inherent in my adolescent genes. Told Mom and Dad I got bad genes from a bad deal.

Penny said I wasn't really bad. She said I'd grow up to be a nice person. She believed that.

Believed in me. Penny was the only one.

My sister.

My best friend.

I tried to repent, felt full of contrition, knew my sins were not overlooked. Told Them I was sorry, truly sorry, so very, very sorry. Make me suffer, I told Them, but don't make Penny suffer.

Hello?

Sobbing...choking...tears in my throat...a gob of tears. Rolled up. Wadded up. Piece of junk.

Throw it away, the piece of junk...

"No!"

"Here. Take this pill. Sandy, sit up. I want you to swallow this pill."

"Not junk. I'm not junk."

"Don't spit. I'm putting the pill in your mouth. Don't spit it out. Now take a sip of water, Sandy! Don't spit the water. Swallow it. Let me see. Open your mouth."

Kat jumped off the bed and ran away. Too much noise. I'd put a stop to that.

"Farmer John's disturbing the peace," I said.

"That pill will take effect in half an hour. You'll feel better."

"Maybe we should crash the party."

"I've got to work the lower field today. Has to be plowed before it rains or it'll be too muddy. C'mon, I'll help you into the living room. Afternoon soaps will be on soon and you can catch up with your stories."

"I hate the television chair. It's a trap, trying to keep me down, makes me struggle to get up. I won't sit in it. Won't wear socks. Won't wear bibs."

"Sandy, now hush a minute. Listen to me. I've got work in the lower fields. You're going to be alone for a few hours and I want you to stay quiet. No wandering around the house. I've put the television on for you. You can watch your soap opera shows. Okay?"

"Okay." Mom assisted me to the sofa and waited until I was seated quietly.

I watched television for a few minutes, but the volume kept creeping up until it was blasting in my head. Mom said she wanted me to stay quiet. How could I stay quiet with the volume out of control?

Alphabet sheets.

I had a project waiting. Project on the back burner. Had to concentrate, pull it closer, flash it on the screen so I could remember what it was.

Had to think. Grab something, anything. Find a clue.

I went to my room and sat at my desk, stared at the dictionary and the notebook. And the pencil. And the words scribbled sloppily on the first line: Dear Sandy.

I remembered.

Mark's letter was folded secretively between the pages of the dictionary and Penny's alphabet sheets were stacked in an orderly pile next to it.

Something was wrong with this picture. The alphabet sheets weren't there before. Someone put them there.

Had to push it aside. Farmer John's party was too loud, and though I'd switched it off, audio from the television continued to echo.

Felt a nap creeping in.

What was this? Silence!

Lovely, peaceful, melodic silence.

When I opened my eyes it was afternoon. I went to Penny's bedroom window and scanned the field until I spotted Dad's tractor moving slowly with Mom at the wheel. My mind seemed unusually free of clutter. I noticed this while I stood staring through the glass and realized an urgency to get busy translating sentences from the cipher letter.

It was hard work deciphering alphabet code, but I made a lot of headway copying Mark's words into my notebook:

Dear Sandy,

otG mlfyse in prsion. Cplaou nem I saw
rugnnin pgesacka for bib emos drit Babge nem
dinnep it no em. Wans't em put ffstu in meht
pgesacka. ssA seloh, the babge nem. Alsyaw get
the wrong nam. You wonk woh it is, kdi.
yeH kdi, the famyli now't rwite em, tel em
wonk hwat's pu dnuora ohme. rWite em a rettel,
Sandy, peek em depost. You wonk em. Just in the
ongwr acepl at the stwor emit. You unstander?
Tell ryou lksfo bna ousicn Penny elloh.
I extecp to de auto here in a reay. You
rwite em. inA't dobyon lese nnaog. Mark.

Once the transfers were complete I worried my eyes trying to figure out what they meant. Recognized a few, but out of context they didn't make sense. I'd have to use the alphabet sheets again.

It was nearing sunset. I returned to Penny's window and surveyed the hundreds of freshly plowed rows of soil. In the distance a tiny pair of tractor headlights showed Mom the way to make even more fresh rows. I was hungry. Not likely she'd be coming back to fix my supper.

In the refrigerator I found a bowl of cabbage and a jar of olives. I dropped some of the olives on the cabbage and ate it while standing over the sink. Without my bib.

Tasted funny, not like the suppers Mom prepared, but it filled the vacancy in my stomach.

I looked around for Kat. Guessed she was out with Mom. I remembered another cat Penny once had. It loved to hang around the borders of freshly plowed fields where mice ran amok.

It would catch the scurrying, fleeing rodents and crush their skulls flat with one quick crunch. Kat was such a good soldier. I would have to introduce her to some of them one day—the boys in blue and the boys in grey. They'd like my Kat. Hoped I would remember. Hoped I could remember.

16

Warm summer mornings lingered, but afternoons were replaced by weather with a crisp chill. Sweater weather. Reminded me of something important I did every year about this time.

An activity?

A chore?

A project? Already had one of those.

Overloads stressed my grey cells and gave me headaches. Wouldn't worry about it. Still had Mark's letter to decipher and one day I would figure it out and write him back. Couldn't do it right away, however, because I was too busy helping Mom with her letters. It was my job and I wasn't complaining, but there were so many letters to decode. Never realized Mom got so much mail. She said it was primarily junk mail, yet I couldn't bother about content. I was too preoccupied with return addresses.

"Mail's coming," I yelled from my chair in the front yard where I positioned myself approximately the same time every afternoon. I could see a segment of the main road as it wound down Pine Top Hill towards the crop fields belonging to our neighbor, farmer John. It was there I always glimpsed the red, white, and blue postal truck making its way to our mailbox.

"Bring it all to me first," Mom called from the garden. She put great emphasis on the word all.

Guess because I sometimes dropped mail in the

driveway trying to get it safely home and Mom had a problem with the delay. Not too many days in the delay. Four at the most. That was the telephone bill. I dropped it on a Friday, it rained during the weekend, and I spotted it while carrying Monday's mail to the house. Mom was upset to an excess. Said she couldn't read the amount due because of water smudges. I told her since the bill was ruined she shouldn't have to pay it. She yelled at me, said "Don't be an idiot."

I thought, I'm not an idiot. Her anger kind of hurt my feelings, but that was all right because Mom had her problems and it was my job to help, not hinder.

And so that's what I was doing this day, helping.

I'd learned to remain seated until the carrier actually stopped at the mailbox because it was a good sign there'd be something in the box when I made my trip down the driveway. It was a very useful piece of information and I often shared it with Mom. "Saves exactly seven hundred and fifty steps," I'd say. I knew because I always counted while traveling to and from the box. Of course, variations were to be expected; sometimes I fell down.

Now I strained to listen in time to hear the postal truck slow, then stop. I recognized the squeak and creak made by the rusted hinges on our box. When the truck drove off, I commenced my journey, remembering to count. Upon returning, letters in hand, I saw Mom standing behind my lawn chair.

"How do you manage counting your steps?" she asked.

"I start with the first," I replied, "and then I count every time one of my feet touches the ground."

"Let me hear you count."

"I have to be walking, going to the mailbox."

"Okay. Let's go to the mailbox."

"Already went," I said, handing Mom the letters. "See? Didn't drop any, either. I was careful."

Mom smiled and winked and took the letters, stuck them into her pocket, then insisted, "I want to hear you count. Seems like a very big number, seven hundred and fifty."

Mom was obviously skeptical and I obliged.

I sat, then rose, and began: "One, two, three, four, five, six, seven, eight, nine, ten, eleven, nineteen, fifteen, fifty, twenty-one..."

"That's very good," Mom said before we were out of the yard. "Do you count the same way every day?"

"You're interrupting. Now I'm mixed up. I have to go back and start over."

"Look what I found in the garden," she said, pointing at the basket full of vegetables near her boot-clad feet.

I leaned into the basket and inspected: "Food."

"Notice anything special?"

Leaning closer, I lost my balance and tumbled forward, smacking my forehead hard against the basket.

"Ouch," Mom mumbled, kneeling to examine my head.

"I'm fine," I said, crawling with difficulty to my wobbling feet.

"Wait. Let me see your noggin."

"Mom! I'm not Chinese!"

Mom seemed surprised. "What's being Chinese got to do with bumping your head?"

"I'm not Chinese 'cause I don't break into smithereens."

Mom's face grew extremely quizzical.

"You know what I mean," I said.

She shook her head.

I was feeling impatient with her ignorance. "You know. Like glass. Like the dishes you never let us use."

"Oh! You mean porcelain China!"

I had to roll my eyes. Mom could sure be dense sometimes. "That's what I already said!"

"I understand," she said smiling. "Now I can't remember what I was doing." "You were giving me today's mail. Didn't lose any?"

I shook my head and thought, If I lost one, how would I know?

She said, "Good for you."

Now I glanced at the basket of vegetables. Two beautiful golden ears of sweet corn were nestled amongst more common garden items. "Corn-on-the-cob! Yum!"

"Yum!" Mom agreed. "Can you guess what we're having for supper?"

I thought about it a few seconds. "Why can't we have corn-on-the-cob?"

Mom grinned, "You want these now?" She pulled the letters from her pocket.

"Okay," I said. "I've got some time on my schedule. I'll go see who they're from."

My deciphering work was interesting, and every day I could tell that my mind was getting quicker at cracking the mysterious alphabet cryptography. Where I once spent an hour with one return address, I could now complete three. Not bad, considering many of the alphabet letters were printed backwards to add confusion. But like I said, I was quick and I caught on to the reversal trick pretty fast.

In fact, I was getting so good at this, I decided it was time to tackle Mark's letter. Three words at a time. Same as I did with Mom's letters.

I cleared my desk top of everything except Mark's letter, the dictionary, a pencil, and notebook paper. Mom had taped Penny's alphabet sheets across the wall in front of my desk, simplifying matters even more.

Turning to a clean page in my notebook, I wrote "Dear Sandy" on the first line and put a check mark next to each word. The check marks reminded me I'd already deciphered these. Going to the second line I wrote "otG"; on the third line I wrote "mlfyse"; on the fourth line I wrote "in"; and on the fifth line I wrote "prsion". That was the entire first sentence in the letter's body. I thought, This is brilliant! Now all I had to do was look each word up and use the alphabet sheets to phonetically sound out the definitions provided by the dictionary. Truly brilliant.

Maybe I could be a spy.

Get paid.

Get paid for what?

I could fold clothes.

Batter up!

Brain-fade sliding off base.

Strike one!

I was tired.

Strike two!

I deserved to rest.

Strike three! You're out!

I hated this game. Who put this game in my head?

Give me a blank slate to play with.

Please lift the pressure before my skull splits. I have a very bad headache. Want to cry. Mom said not to wait until the hurting consumes me. Doctor Rheis gave Mom pills so she wouldn't feel this pain.

"Mom!"

Don't scream.

"Mom!"

Don't scream. Please. The sounds echo; truly painful.

"Help!"

Mom's fingers pried my mouth open, forced a pill to the back of my throat. Almost gagged me.

"Drink this water," Mom said.

I could smell the corn boiling. My absolute favorite, corn-on-the-cob. Would have a piece for supper. With lots of salt and butter. Kat would want some butter. She'd know all that butter was melting between the kernels and she'd want her share. Kat liked butter almost as much as she liked a spot of coffee with her cream.

Where was Kat? Couldn't remember.

Couldn't remember what day it was.

I had been sleeping a lot. Every time Mom made me eat pills I slept. Seemed like I was sleeping too much. Someone once said, "This is the first day of the rest of your life." A person shouldn't sleep through that first day.

17

Early the following morning I heard the school bus and I remembered what happened every year when summer afternoons grew cool.

"Mom! School started! Mom!"

I scrambled from my bed in too much of a hurry to walk and found myself crawling into Penny's room. I reached for the windowsill and pulled myself up in time to see the imposing machine disappear on the ribbon of road over Pine Top. It passed my house never even slowing to see if I was late.

"Mom! I missed the bus!"

Mom was standing in Penny's doorway shaking her head. Seemed she shook her head at me a lot these days.

"You'll have to take me in the car to catch up with the bus."

Mom frowned.

"What should I wear? It's the first day of school! I should wear something new. Do I have any new clothes? Did we shop for new clothes? I can't remember. Can you remember?"

Mom sighed and left without answering. Guess because she couldn't remember, either. I went to my closet, sorted through dresses on hangers and skirts folded on the shelf. The skirts seemed a bit messy so I carefully removed and refolded each one. While folding I noticed a stain on my favorite tweed.

Would need to soak it out. Penny always washed the wools. It was a special procedure, requiring soap in a pink bottle Penny stored in the cabinet beneath the bathroom sink.

I found the soap, filled the sink with lukewarm water and tried to read the directions on the bottle. Impossible. The words were microscopic; I'm positive I could've read everything easily if the print had been larger.

"Sandy!" Mom yelled from the kitchen.

"What?"

"I made a bowl of oatmeal for you. Come in here and eat your breakfast."

"I'm busy," I yelled back.

Now what? I examined the bottle. That didn't help. I could simply pour soap in until it bubbled.

"Measure with the cap," Penny whispered over my shoulder.

"Penelope!" I turned to hug her and tell her how much I missed her living at home.

"Who're you talking to?" Mom was standing out in the hall peering in.

"You know."

"No. Tell me."

"Penny. She was here a second ago. Is she in the kitchen?"

Mom breathed heavily before saying, "Penny isn't in the kitchen."

"Oh. Wonder where she went." I removed the bottle cap, filled it with soap, poured the soap into the basin and splashed the water until suds appeared. Next I immersed the section of skirt with the stain and rubbed it with my finger tips until the stain began to lift out.

"You're doing a real good job with that," Mom

said.

"Yeah."

"I looked into your room. See you've got your skirts laid out on the floor. Are you cleaning your closet?"

"Mom?"

"Yes?"

"I thought classes always started at the university before we went back to regular school."

"That's right."

"Why isn't Penny in Knoxville?"

"Maybe she had a short break."

"Oh."

"Oatmeal is getting cold."

"Did you put milk and sugar on it?"

"Of course."

"Where's Kat?"

"I don't know. Around here somewhere. Why?"

"I think I'd rather have dry cereal."

"Suit yourself."

"Where can I hang my skirt to dry?"

"Hand it to me. I'll lay it on a towel in the laundry room."

"Okay."

"Now let's go eat some breakfast."

"Wait. I should check my other skirts, see if I can find any more stains."

"You've got all day to do that."

"Okay...oops...okay...no...you wait."

"Now what?"

"Remember? School started today. I saw the bus. I've got to get dressed and you'll have to take me."

Mom hesitated before saying, "You aren't going back to school."

I was dumbfounded. My mother, the same woman who believed the only way to get into Heaven was with a high school diploma, was telling me I didn't have to go to school.

"But this is my senior year."

"I need you to stay home with me."

"Oh. Well. Okay. Why?"

"I...well, I need you to stay home and...and help out. You've seen all the work I have to do everyday, now that your father's gone."

"Penny, too," I reminded her.

"What?"

"Me and Penny used to share chores. Now I'll have to do both my work and Penny's, right? I don't mind, Mom. I'm glad Penny got her scholarship. I don't mind doing my work and Penny's work."

"It'll be okay," Mom promised. "Things will work out and next year, we'll see."

"Next year I'll finish my senior year and graduate."

When my cereal bowl was empty I set my dishes in the sink and went to my room. Mom was gone and wouldn't be home until after dark. She did this occasionally, took off for the day. Never said where she was going or what she was doing, but I knew. The evening before these trips she always carried her sewing basket out to the car. Thought I didn't notice. I noticed. Probably earning a bit of money doing alterations for a dress shop or a local tailor. Mom was good with a needle and thread and I was proud of her. But I guessed why she didn't say anything. Most of my life I'd been angry with no particular target. Anger doesn't always need a target, it diffuses around nicely without one.

Back to the sewing basket. During my first year

in high school, I remembered, the debutante types always needed a special new dress for this party or that event. Not me. I hung out in graveyards with my friends, drinking a few beers. Why graveyards? Because the debutante types never came to graveyards.

What was I getting at? Oh yeah. The sewing basket. Well, that's what Mom was doing, sewing party outfits for the debutante types. She actually went to these people's houses and they always advised her to use the back door. Like a servant.

Made me angry.

Embarrassed.

Ashamed.

Wished I could say, "Mom, I'm proud of you. I know you're a wonderful seamstress." Wished I could say, "I apologize for all my anger." Wished I could say, "I wish I was more like Penny." Penny always told Mom she was proud of her.

Didn't want to waste time thinking about things that made me feel bad about myself. Besides, my right ear was hurting. Couldn't imagine why it hurt. Deep inside my head I felt the sting followed by a throbbing hollow misery at the root of the ear canal. Needed something to do, a nice distraction. Would have less time to worry about my ear if my feet were busy.

Good trick. Trick my ear with busy feet.

Could go for a walk in the woods.

"Where'd you come from?" he asked anxiously, jumping to his feet and clutching his rifle.

"From my house," I replied. "You're one of the grey fellows. I recognize your uniform." The recognition made me feel especially perceptive. I made a note in my mind about paying more attention to people's uniforms.

"Southern Independents," he said, throwing out his chest and posturing proud. "Where's your house?" he asked.

"Over thataway."

"Ain't seen no house down there."

I shrugged, "Must not've looked real hard."

"No," he was shaking his head, "I woulda seen a house. Hey, what happened to your face?"

"Nothing."

"Looks like somebody busted you good."

"Nobody busted me. I've been in a few fights but I never got beat, understand? Say, why're you here by yourself? Don't you guys usually travel in bunches?"

"Got separated."

"Maybe you deserted."

"I said I got separated."

"Whatever. Where're you going?"

"Place called Corinth. You heard of it?"

"Of course I've heard of Corinth. Everybody around here's been to Corinth."

"You know Grant took Paducah, Fort Henry and Fort Donelson?"

"Is that bad?"

"Kentucky's fallen. T'was with Bolivar's army when Grant ordered 'unconditional and immediate surrender'. Barely escaped with m'life."

"How'd you manage?"

"Crawled through a muddy creek for a coupla miles. Nearly froze to death."

"Why're you going to Corinth?"

"Heard rumor Polk and Johnston were headin' that direction."

"Is that good?"

"You bet."

"Well," I said, glancing up at the clear sky, "seems like this is good traveling weather."

"That it is. Pleased to meet you, Miss," he tilted his hat, "but I best be movin' along, now. God be with you...and... well...God be with you."

I stood in the middle of the trail and watched his back while he hiked southward. "Good luck," I yelled. He raised an arm and waved without turning around. For an instant I wanted to run and catch up with him, accompany him down to Corinth. But something told me he was going to die in Corinth.

"Too young," I muttered, picking up a stick. It was a sturdy, strong stick and it helped me maintain balance while I kept my feet busy.

"Too young to die in Corinth," I sang, adding a melodic chorus of humming while poking my finger into my ear, chasing the pain through the tunnel and keeping my feet busy.

18

Mom was going to be pleased when she returned. I fixed and devoured my lunch without leaving a single crumb on the floor or anywhere else in the kitchen, and I did it all without messing up dishes.

Such a brilliant idea. Required my cleverness to pluck it out of nothingness and make it workable. Indeed, these days I was capable of profound thoughts when I least expected them. It was ever so simple. I took two pieces of bread, put them flat on the counter, and used my finger to scoop peanut butter and jelly out of the jar and spread it on the bread. Next I licked the peanut butter and jelly off my finger and ate while leaning over the sink. All my crumbs fell into the sink!

Flawless!

Well.

Almost flawless.

Would've been flawless except for the chewing. Chewing made my ear throb. Wished I could make food slide down my throat without chewing. Might be worth a try; but what if I choked? Didn't imagine I'd enjoy choking.

I removed myself to the front yard for a nap in the sunshine while awaiting the post. When it finally arrived it didn't. The truck didn't stop. I knew from experience that meant there would be zilch in the mailbox.

Now my afternoon was a goose egg and I was

sure to be bored.

I hated vast expanses of nothingness.

Hated continuance of less than the total of zero.

This was making me hostile and agitated and really, really riled. I could feel a tantrum settling in; could visualize a darned good rampage smack dab in the middle of the front yard. Throwing rocks. Slinging insults. Breaking lawn furniture. Could easily see me draining all the water from the birdbath and watching with satisfied contentment while birds pretended to splash themselves in a pool of...nothing.

That wouldn't be fair and might actually be unkind. One could even say such behavior was crazy and cruel.

I wasn't crazy and didn't believe I'd ever been cruel. Penny would defend me. She'd stand in my corner defending my many virtues while listing numerous good deeds which she'd swear were all of my doing.

And once again, as she always did, my sister would save me from myself. Or perhaps for once I could save myself by not throwing a tantrum.

Take a walk, a voice suggested. Not my voice. Didn't recognize it and was about to ignore it when it repeated: Take a walk. Seemed like an idea I might've had on my own, so I walked.

I walked first in circles around the yard. When this activity served to make me dizzy, I ventured off down the driveway. Straight-line strolling. Straightening out the circles which knotted up my thoughts, bewildered my eyes and confounded my feet.

I discovered I couldn't count steps in a circle. My feet followed one after the other, over and over and over, until I was convinced I was back where I'd begun. But I couldn't be certain. Where does a circle begin?

The driveway was easy. My chair was the beginning and the ending, regardless how many steps I counted. And now I had counted two hundred and sixty-one when I noticed the sun shadowed behind several ominous heavy clouds which commenced to spitting. Within seconds the spit turned downpour and soon I was wet-soaked to total saturation. I couldn't allow the rain to stop me when I was in the middle of a project. Would lose my place if I went back; wouldn't know if the driveway had gotten shorter or longer since last count.

Suddenly a movement caught my attention.

"Hey!" I yelled, waving at the soldier who suddenly appeared at the border of farmer John's cotton field. The field was shallow, probably two acres deep and extremely long, stretching behind a cluster of forest for another twenty or more acres. "Hey!" I yelled again. He seemed deafened by the turbulent stormy shower. I'd have to hurry to the end of the driveway where our gravel lane intersected with the paved county road. Surely he could see me from there if I ran fast, very fast, like I used to run. I used to run all the time. I was good at running.

Had been.

Had once been good at running.

Couldn't seem to recall how it was done. My left foot was reaching out ahead and the right foot followed with lily-livered, feeble hesitations. The familiar unfamiliar voice said, pick up the foot; put down the foot; keep moving the feet.

Keep 'em moving.

Pick 'em up.

Put 'em down.

Move 'em up.

Move 'em down.

Like a herd of little doggies.

Get-a-long, get-a-long.

Left stride, right hop, left stride, right hop.

Like a car with two tires flat on one side, flat on the top.

Klump-plop, klump-plop.

Too much for a herd of little doggies with two flat tires.

Whoa! All them doggies were going out of control, running amok and busting up the herd. No wonder I couldn't remember how to run. My brain was teeming with mischievous voices, disobedient beasts, and broken machines! Didn't matter. Too late. The soldier had disappeared deep into a heavy pine thicket farther up the field. I wondered if he were on his way to Corinth. Maybe he'd meet up with the grey uniform I'd met who insisted he was with the Southern Independents. That'd be nice. They could travel together if they wore the same color uniform. I had been too far away to see if he was a blue or a grey. Of course, if he was a blue and he met up with the other one, they'd probably kill each other.

Nothing I could do about that.

Besides, my ear was in distress again. I hoped Mom would get home soon so I could tell her about my pain. Seemed to make it less intense when I could give some away. Like cookies when I baked up a batch and shared them. Wasn't sure I'd ever baked up a batch of cookies.

Penny liked to bake cookies...and cakes...and bread.

She helped Mom out in the kitchen a lot and she was such a big help and I felt desperately lonely standing there in the dousing, drenching rain, my head swarming with unruly characters and my ear full of misery. If only I could rest; just sit down and rest.

"You're getting wet," Penny said.

"I thought you were away at school!" I said, surprised as I turned to see my sister at my side.

"Why would I want to be at school? I'd rather be here having a walk with you. Where should we go?"

"I'm feeling tired," I said.

"Nonsense. How can you get your strength back if you rest just because you're tired?"

"I guess that makes sense. But my ear tortures me an awful lot these days."

"Let me look," Penny said, parting my hair, peering deep into my ear. "Looks okay to me."

"Really?"

"Yeah."

"Wonder why it hurts so bad?"

Penny seemed to contemplate this for a moment, then she asked, "Did you stuff something into it?"

"No."

"Are you sure?"

"I'm sure."

"Well, if you're sure, but..."

"But what?"

"I remember when you were about four. You stuffed a bean in your nose to see where it would come out."

"Where did it come out?"

"It never came out," Penny sighed. "I'm wondering if maybe that's what's wrong with your ear."

"You think that bean finally worked it's way into my ear?"

"Could be."

"That's awful. Try to see if you can get it out." I held my hair behind my head while Penny prodded my ear in search of the lost bean.

"What if it's sprouting inside your head?"

"That's impossible."

"Hmmmm."

"Don't you think it's impossible?"

Penny shrugged, "It's getting cold. Let's go home and build a fire in the fireplace."

"What's that noise?"

"It's the school bus," Penny said.

"Let's wait for it."

"No. Let's don't."

"It's already here. Wave so they'll see us," I said, watching as it rolled down the road toward our driveway entrance. It passed the entrance, kept on moving. I yelled and flailed my arms about.

"Don't do that," Penny scolded.

"Why?"

"They'll think you're crazy if they see you."

"Why?"

"Because that's what they want to think."

"Oh." By now the bus was out of sight, over the hill. The rain was falling in thick and heavy sheets. "I'm so tired," I said, feeling my knees going weak, collapsing beneath me. I dropped into a heap on the wet gravel and clutched at my ear. It was throbbing severely.

"Sandy!" Mom was yelling, "Sandy! What are you doing?"

I folded myself tighter to keep out the rain.

"Get up!"

Had to tilt my head correctly, make sure all that moisture They were pouring off the Heavens didn't fill my ear and make it worse.

"Enough of this. Now get on your feet. Let's go. Get up! I can't carry you to the car. You're going to have to walk."

"The bean is inside my eardrum, probably rooted through my brain by now." I propelled myself to a standing position and noticed the daylight had turned to darkness and the rain was unrelenting.

"Stop with that nonsense. Pick up your feet. That's right. C'mon. Very good. A few more steps. There!"

I pulled myself into the passenger seat of Mom's car. "It's not raining in here," I observed with relief.

"Of course it isn't. Now sit still." She ran around the car, crawled into the driver's seat, and put the transmission into drive. Within seconds we were delivered to our front porch and she was out of the car again, opening my door, grabbing my arms, forcing me to leave the warm, dry compartment.

When we entered the living room I was disappointed to see the fireplace was cold and bare. "I thought Penny was going to build a fire," I said.

"I'll make a fire." Mom seemed irritated. "Go to your room and put on some dry pajamas and wrap a towel around your head."

"I'm soaked."

"Yes you are! What in the world? Forget it. I don't want to hear. I really, really don't. Go to your room and change."

19

"There's not enough for me to do," I grumbled, sitting on my chair beside the dryer and peering inside. It was empty. I'd folded the last of the laundry, of which there'd been very little. I raised my voice and called, "Mom!"

"What?" she called back.

"There were only three things in the dryer. My shirt, my shorts, and my underwear. That's all there was. I already folded them."

"Good. Now you can get in the kitchen and finish your soup."

I carefully closed the dryer lid so it wouldn't make too much noise and carried my clothes to my bedroom, put them into their proper drawers and returned to have a seat at the kitchen table. "I'm wearing Penny's pajamas," I said.

Mom glanced at me while eating her dinner and nodded.

"They were mixed in with my pajamas."

Mom nodded again before taking another bite of bread.

"I wonder how they got there?"

Mom didn't answer, she just stared at her food and continued chewing.

"My ear is hurting," I said.

"When did that start?"

"Penny said I put a bean in my nose when I was

four and she thinks it finally worked its way into my ear where it might be sprouting and growing."

Mom studied my face for a few seconds, then shook her head and left the kitchen. When she returned she carried one of the tablets she gave me when my head ached. "Swallow this with some milk," she said, placing the yellow disc in my mouth.

Visions loomed in my mind's eye of the curious population residing in my brain and I began wondering if it was waiting for the pill. I pushed the pill under my tongue and swallowed a gulp of milk.

"Do you want to watch television?" Mom asked while clearing her dishes.

"Nope."

"Do you plan on eating anything?"

"Nope."

"Suit yourself."

If I finished my dinner the pill might work its way into my food and down my throat and they-who-populated-my-brain would get it. It was my obligation to deprive them. I searched around with the tip of my tongue to make sure it was still in my mouth.

"What are you doing?" Mom queried, studying my facial distortions.

"Cleaning my teeth."

"Do that with your toothbrush."

I took that as an exit cue and shuffled down the hall to my bedroom. I didn't turn the light on because I didn't want Them watching while I extracted the pill and hid it under my bed.

Next morning when I awoke I found myself scrunched up between my bed and the wall. Kat was asleep in my lap.

Odd. Her little engine wasn't humming. I touched

her furry soft head and scratched behind her ears as gently as I could. Her engine remained silent. Placing the sensitive pad of my index finger across her velvet nose I detected no warmth emitting from her nostrils, no condensed moisture, nor brief quick puffs of air forced out upon exhalation. I sensed nothing.

I scratched behind her ears again. She always liked it when I scratched her kitten ears. She always hummed. She wasn't now.

Insanity or injury? Sometimes it seemed the same. I knew it was there waiting, like a fever, like spent shell casings glistening in the heat across a familiar battle-field.

If I were insane, how would I know? I could feel myself slipping and I didn't want to be alone during the transition.

Hold the fortress!

In the corner of my room Kat and I guarded the fort ever so courageously against the brightness of first morning sun and specks of dancing dusty lint stream-ing down each spray of light. We held fast like sailors with their captain going down with the ship; like troop-ers taking no prisoners.

No prisoners.

Prisoners would populate the cells, those dark damp holes in the ground where the perspiration of all those who went before still clung wearily condemned to the crumbling walls, and I could smell it.

It was waiting! I could feel it staring at me with big hungry eyes, waiting for me to fall into the pit, the cell, the place where they took the dead ones before they went insane!

I was drifting in and out of something so frighten-ing I could almost touch the terror; I could certainly

hear it:
"Take Kat to the basement," they said.
"No!"
"She's gone," they said.
"Pull the curtain wide so I can see the clock!"
"Hush!" they said.
"Help us, please," I cried pathetically. "Kat's engine isn't humming. Can't You make it hum again? You are the best Magician and I know You could if only You would, for me, before the time runs out and I am all alone."

All the sights and sounds of life must have taken holiday for there to be so much of nothing where Kat and I found ourselves hunkered down. We shivered and my flesh turned blue. It was an opaque purple-blue. So well it hid the fleshy sack which housed my brittle bones and syrup blood. And especially Kat's sighs, for there were none. That's how I knew we were alone inside this place which we could not abandon to the enemy. We could not since it was our decision to stay our position until the last drop of blood was spilled into the soil.

It was this same soil that so many believed was worth all the suffering, screaming, crying and dying. It was here they buried their dead six feet in the ground when they had time to dig such an extravagant pit.

I liked it more than the basement, where I believed they laid the dead out in rows to rot away...

"Kat! Penny and I forgot to feed the horses!"

Too late! A couple of trains came together. Collided. It sounded like two locomotives kissing metal, sending exploding slivers of shrapnel everywhere. I really, really didn't want to be alone during this transition.

.

Kat had a very soft voice.

Peaceful, tranquil, serene.

You could not hear her when she sighed.

If Kat was gone I could bury her six feet down beneath the floor where we sat with our wounds, where we suffered. If I buried her perhaps she would cease to suffer. But if she was gone I'd be alone.

Kat couldn't be gone! I kept her safe and well nourished. I shared my oatmeal and Mom's richly creamed coffee. I shared all that she needed and I was never cruel.

But I was cruel to them, the odd fellows who populated my head. It was with premeditation that I refused them their pill the evening before. They caused me a night of fitful distress and left me pivoting on a spindle of wretched torment while I tried to fight them off, keep them from stealing my mind.

I shut out the light and made my room dungeon dark, but my eyes filled their sockets and stared owl-like into spaces not yet occupied. My eyes stared so hard that some of my hair fell out.

But I could not force slumber. Not in my bed, not on the floor, not laying prone, supine, fetal. Not standing or sitting. I did not sleep until the end. I am sure that is when they slipped out through my very sore ear and crawled beneath my bed to snatch the yellow disc.

Kat must have witnessed this act of thievery, and it was them, I am sure, who cast the spell that stole away her engine.

She would want me to bury her in this incredibly rich soil which was valuable beyond life itself since so many fought for the right to die here. Kat was going to enjoy her wondrous newfound wealth.

First I would have to dig through this hard floor.

With my hands.

Using my fingernails.

It was a very hard floor, but I had to keep digging until I reached dirt and burrowed in at least six feet. The richness of so much valuable dirt boggled my mind and spurred me into a frenzy of eagerness to get to it quickly. Carpet threads with their rubber-tough backing gave way more easily than polished cedar planks; but I was forced to persevere in spite of the splintery slivers which worked deep beneath my nails, and in spite of the increasing drops of life syrup which stained everything blood red. I ripped and tore, scratched and clawed, and knew with certainty I was getting closer to the bountiful earth.

"Oh-my-God-Sandra!"

It was a familiar voice but I didn't have time to stop for conversational chit-chat. I said, "Too busy. Go away."

"You-are-tearing-your-hands!"

Arms as familiar as the voice lifted me off the floor and kept me suspended so that I could not continue my project. It was an interesting suspension, and I decided I might fly if I stretched my arms wide like a soaring eagle.

"What's wrong? Sandra! Sandra? Can you hear me?"

I let my arms go limp at my sides and found myself once again crouched on the floor. Immediately I resumed my digging, more earnestly now than before.

"Sandy! What's the matter with you?"

"Said I'm really busy and thought I made it clear."

The hands gripped my shoulders with a firmness that hurt and I tried to shrug them off. That seemed to agitate them into a fit of violence and they began furiously shaking me.

They were the angriest hands in the world. Shaking and shaking and shaking me. It was a horrible dizzying feeling, this shaking, and I believed—quite truly feared—it would not stop until my brain drained from my tortured ear. With frantic urgency I held my head and tried desperately to make it cease before the horror devoured all my senses. Before there would be nothing left but the terror.

"He cut it out of his life!" I cried.

"What?"

"His ear was a nuisance so he cut it out of his life."

The hands released me seconds before my demise.

"Who are you talking about? What are you talking about?"

I groped around for something solid and focused until I could see Mom sitting on her heels in front of me. She seized my wrists in a vice grip, kept them away from the floor.

"Van Gogh. Vincent Van Gogh took a sharp knife—or maybe it was a dull knife—and he sliced his ear, Mom. Sliced it completely away. So it couldn't hurt him anymore. And then he sent it to his friend Paul. If you would get me a knife I could slice this off, but I don't know who I could mail it to, maybe Mark. I could mail it to Mark." I pulled my hands free and began tearing at my ear lobe. Mom quickly restrained me, pinning my hands between hers.

"Is that why you did this?" Mom asked, examining the damaged floor with punishing eyes.

I stared at the mess I'd made. "This is for Kat."

"What's wrong with Kat?"

I jerked my hands from her grasp and reached beneath my bed, gently lifted my little friend and held her out for Mom.

20

"Where in the world did you get poison?" Mom demanded.

"Huh?"

"You know exactly what I mean! What kind of poison did you put in your room! And what the hell were you trying to kill?"

Poison? I couldn't imagine why I'd do that. I stared at Mom, dumbfounded. Kat was sick and she needed us, and Mom was too busy acting weird. It was all adding up to another headache.

"I think I'm gonna barf," I said.

"Shut up! Now I'm going to ask you once more. Where did you get poison, where are you hiding it, and what the hell do you need it for?"

"I swear," I said, crossing my heart, "I don't have any poison."

"Kat got poison from somewhere and now she's dead!"

"Kat? poisoned? No. Not Kat. Kat's just sick."

"Kat's dead!"

Mom seemed to be accusing me. I shook my head until the extra motion made me dizzy and aggravated the nausea I was already experiencing.

"This is exactly something I can see the new you doing!" Mom said, her tone hostile. When she said this she said it with such enormous conviction that I wandered around inside my thoughts and wondered what happened to the old me.

"Where is the other one?" I asked just as she launched into an oration of ranting and raving, scolding and fuming, cursing and growling, as if she'd been born angry. She was, in my humble opinion, carrying herself into obsessive territory.

"Where?" I asked, emphasizing the words, "Where is the other one?"

Her lips stopped moving and I noted the bitter diatribe which she had been spewing forth without taking the time even to breath or inhale or replenish her lungs between syllables ceased. She looked at me as if I had only recently arrived. It made me aware she was looking at the new me. The one she accused of poisoning Kat. The entire idea distressed me, made me want to break and run, tear up the ground with flying feet which moved so fast they could out-distance this new issue. This new me. This possible imposter who was capable of distributing poison around my room. But I knew she was wrong about the poison and about Kat.

It must be a spell. There wasn't any poison and had never been any poison. I believed it was them. The characters inside my head. They put a spell on Kat.

I was more confused than ever and I imagined Mom would be confused too if I tried to explain.

Just then Mom asked, "What other one?"

I detected impatience in her tone, but it was impatience tinged with sanity.

"Huh?"

"You wanted to know where the other one was," she said.

"You know," I whispered, glancing around the room, in case the other one was listening. "The other one who you thought was me. It is...terribly confusing."

Silence.
Prolonged, lengthy silence.
"Mom?"
"Yes?"
"Are you confused?"
Suddenly Mom began to weep with an intensity I'd never before witnessed and it seemed all the sorrow of her life was on stage. I was frightened watching her facial tissue swell until her entire head bubbled and bloated. She was definitely unhappy. I was unhappy too, but I didn't believe we could rescue Kat from the spell of malicious Tricksters by sobbing our guts out.

With a careful, gentle love I carried Kat away from Mom, away from the house, away from the encompassing shroud of obsession. ,Shielding her tiny kitten form, so fragile and trusting, within the cradle of my arms, we journeyed far into the woods. ,It was uphill much of the time. , We moved toward a place where I knew she would be safe, a place where nothing worse could ever happen. Nothing worse than everything which had gone before: every dangerous thing, like war and poison and loneliness. We were tired of it all.

While we traveled the pain in my head pushed through the center of my brain like a hot branding iron searing everything in its path. I winced and groaned but tried to ignore it since we could not break the count of steps in our journey. Not to rest our sorry bones even when our bodies creaked and cried out for mercy. Not to find water for sipping and quenching the thirst in our dehydrated souls. Not for any reason. We could not.

We made tracks through pine-topped hills which greedily groped for the heavens with their sharp needle boughs while we left prints deep in soggy brackish bottoms which smelled strong of decay and rotted things

too numerous to mention. It was a great distance we
would have to cover if we were to reach this place in
time.

It was a difficult trek because of the sultry humidity which continued to squash our pores so we
would feel every sweltering degree of the day. And
because Penny's pajamas were made from heavy cotton
fabric.

Pajamas were not good traveling garb.

I could shed them in the forest.

Let my fanny moon the trail.

And find myself humiliated when we reached
our special place? No way. I would endure, suffocating
beneath the cloth which ripped everytime I passed too
close to briar brambles and wild berry bushes. I would
endure the scratches and abrasions which now decorated my hide like medallions won in battle. The battle.
The one we journeyed towards as we followed Snake
Creek until it merged with Owl Creek. And when the
waters mixed we searched until we discovered the foot-
prints made by tens of thousands of men, thousands of
horses and hundreds of wagons pulling guns—loud
and noisy, deadly, mutilating machines prepared and
ready for war—traveling along the Hamburg-Savannah
Road.

Once on the road I allowed my bare feet to fall
only upon prints already stamped into the earth. This
earth, home of the special killing ground where so many
yearned to die amidst the butchery and carnage of their
very own holocaust.

It gave me new energy which I badly needed
after having traveled more than half a day to reach this
site. I lifted Kat to my face and kissed her sweet fur and
then I hugged her close to my heart and hurried, reluc-

tantly dragging my cowardly weak leg, since there was nothing else to do with it.

When I heard the first shot and felt the rush of air as a shell burst over my head, I knew I had arrived in time. I made my way to the familiar landmark: Shiloh Church. It was the center place for all that was to come. And it was coming, surging forward, crashing out from the forest surrounding us. Rebel troops rushed into the open field, surprising the Federal troops while they breakfasted, and all Hell spilled forth upon the earth as far as eyes could see.

A rabbit fled the brush nearby and scurried in circles, frightened into abnormal behavior, until it found a dead soldier and snuggled close to him for safety.

Meanwhile cannon fire drew my attention and I turned to see two commanders ordering their rebel troops to launch an attack across the clearing in front of the Sunken Road. As soon as the men were into the open field, another rebel brigade drew up and simply watched while the others formed long lines and began trotting towards a split-rail fence. They could not know, but I could see the Yankees lying down behind the fence. There they waited until the rebels reached cannon range, and then they opened fire while a chorus contributed cross fire. The rebels fell right and left while the wind blew ripples through the tall grass which covered the field as if nothing was happening.

But there were no birds to sing melodies while the wind whipped the grass, and I realized it wasn't wind that moved the grass, it was men falling.

Those in the field who weren't dead were wounded. Some less seriously, and I watched while they continued to charge the split-rail fence and the rows of Yankees. They came on, running faster and faster and faster, directly into the fire from hundreds of rifles, until their charge was entirely destroyed.

Opposite this field more Confederates came to fight. They ran beyond and behind the split-rail fence and began routing out the Yankees until all was chaos. It seemed a million hornets were turned loose in the dozen or more open fields surrounding the log chapel, for there was a buzzing of such frantic nature, I was certain I'd never heard anything like it. While distracted by the buzzing, a horseman approached me from the direction of the head ravines of Oak Creek, a mire bottom bordered by ridges and wet only after a heavy rain. It was wet now and his horse's legs were coated thick with marsh mud. I worried that the horse might not have been fed well, when quite suddenly the horseman shouted and rose tall in his saddle. Something struck behind his cheek and rapidly penetrated his head, exiting through his eye. He cried out and fell from his horse. I glanced around for witnesses and found thousands. Yet surely there was not one who cared. So with a free hand I grabbed the horse by his reins and claimed him.

Sometime afterwards I recognized the buzzing did not come from a hornet's nest. It was caused by hostile bullets and scourging cannon balls which bombarded skirmish lines in all directions. Troops advanced and fell back, assorted officers galloped their stallions in disorganized frenzies, and it was obvious to me neither the blue nor the grey had thought to bring litter-bearers or medical care-givers. Men from both sides died terribly, scattered across hundreds and hundreds of acres. Some lay mortally wounded, screaming and begging for water to quench the thirst caused by gun-shot holes in their broken bodies.

"Water! Please, some water!" their voices cried until They heard them and the sky opened and They poured rain across the ghastly scene.

I coveted Kat close to my chest and tightly clutched my new horse's rein while making my way over the dying and dead. We followed Lick Creek as we journeyed to the Tennessee River. The rain fell hard and we passed several thousand stragglers who took cover beneath the river's bluffs. They all appeared panicked and beaten, regardless of their uniform color. Once we came upon a general who was busy berating his troops, trying to bully them into battle. He threatened to have gunboats from the river turn their shells upon these bluffs but the soldiers ignored him. I was surprised he thought they would care since the shells of gunboats were only shells, and already they had more than plenty overhead.

When we reached the river it was swollen from the torrents of rain and the water was deep in the ravines. Several gunboats patrolled the banks and fired every fifteen minutes. I ignored them and found a fair shelter beneath a tree for me and Kat and my horse.

And it was there we waited beside the river that ran red with blood on this April-bloody-April.

21

I was feeling especially lucid, clever and clear-headed standing here on the banks of the Tennessee River alongside a road which was in almost impassable condition due to the heavy rains from the previous days and nights. The sun was just rising when a Confederate regiment came into view. They appeared to have emerged straight from Hell and looked all the worse for their experience. Some wore physical injuries. All bore wounds of the spiritual type while they dragged their artillery and supply trains over roads of ankle-deep mud, making them more difficult for troops following later. They were met by another Confederate division, one rested and ready in proud form as if prepared for review. When the two came together in the slush-soggy mud, the retreating regiment dropped much of their artillery, then continued on. There were no words exchanged. No greetings, no conversation of any nature. Only the artillery connected them—for a brief moment—and even that connection was severed when the stragglers kept moving farther and farther away, until all that remained was the abandoned stuff of war.

The artillery.

Used and dirty.

Soiled by so much maiming and killing.

And killing...

They—this fresh division—did not want the artillery. They did not hurry to pick it up. Instead they stood there stuck in the mud, staring at all the stuff, until finally one stooped low enough to touch the business end of a cannon. As he did this a battery of Federal troops emerged from the ravine and charged with fire as rapid and accurate as any I'd seen. The rebels were sorely outnumbered and I watched while their parade was shattered. The few who did not die quickly fell and then died slowly. I heard their moans and cries and I remembered, war is hell. I knew war. I knew it as well as any here.

Here on the banks of this river running red.

Red as blood.

Where the sunshine lit up the sky and competed with the flashes of remarkable brightness made by fighting men and their fighting machines. So much light blinded me. I squeezed the reins of my newly acquired horse, hugged Kat firmly with my free arm, and began making my way across the ridges and through the creeks and into the open fields. I had to return to the log chapel, the Shiloh Church. That is where They would be.

I wanted Them to witness how well I cared for Kat, how carefully I cradled her small form-without-its-engine humming.

I didn't poison Kat. I would never do something so horrible and cruel. Such a foul deed; I wouldn't and couldn't do a thing as mean as that. I proved how much I cared. I proved it by bringing her here to this battle of battles, this place where I had played most of my life. Played at battle. Played at play. Played at being. This place where the Devil had His day so near my home and my heart and my soul.

And now that Kat was a war veteran as well she

would be readily welcomed by these soldiers. They would be pleased to meet her and they would be proud to take her with them to that place where all the soldiers go when the battles are won and the wars are over and the wounds...bleed...forever...

22

The wounds bleed forever.

And we wait...

The assault lasts for several hours more, but gradually it becomes clear the greys are too disorganized to rally, and the blues are too many in number to rally against.

It is time for the greys to retire from this contest.

Several stragglers pass us seeming not to notice our presence until one at the rear lifts his weary eyes and smiles. I approach him and extend my arms to reveal the small form of Kat. He takes her from me and raises her to his shoulder.

While he leaves, I watch Kat's small ears perk up and I see her wide kitten eyes are open. She is watching me grow smaller as the distance between us expands.

And I can hear her little engine humming.

It seems odd and out of sorts with the natural order of things, but the air is—all at once and within the same unit of time—kissed by a dry sunny breeze and smothered by the heavy humidity of a stormy day. My nostrils fill with the aroma of fresh-cut lawn and with the sweet stench of so much spilled blood that I begin to feel sick. I am wondering where I am and how I arrived in this place of spontaneous opposites.

If I sit quietly the answers will come, and perhaps the voices which crowd my mind and sound like the screeching of ten thousand wounded souls will subside. But who are these ghosts that haunt me night and day? Haunt me in my wake and in my slumber? It doesn't seem to make a difference to them. Maybe if I find them, or the one which I remember meeting as it came at me on a wind from Hell and swept me into a sea of decayed wars and souls too wounded to drift on.

The banshee.

That was the one. I am suddenly so sure of what I remember I fear my certainty might overwhelm me until all traces of me vanish and I am only a memory.

Like Kat.

Like Penny.

I am afraid.

Me and my newly acquired horse are tired and thirsty as we stumble across the vast field which surrounds us. I don't sense surprise or even curiosity when I recognize a man sprawled supine. He introduced himself at the hospital, it seemed ages earlier. Then, as now, he was wearing a grey jacket and grey slacks with a stripe at the side. A curly red beard swallows his pale featureless face and strands of his equally curly hair spread on the ground around him like a halo. I approach him and fall to my knees beside him. A wound the size of my fist exposes pieces of his rib cage while the bountiful earth greedily consumes the fluid which was his life.

"Ben O'Riley, farewell," I say, and then I gently pull his eyelids down until he appears peaceful in sleep.

When I stand again, glancing about in every direction, I cannot see the horse. I can see the Federals and Confederates wearing their burial suits of blue and grey. All of them are so real I can touch their suffering and hold their pain close. I don't want to let go. It reminds me how I was unable to release Penny's hand the day the curtain fell across my world.

"But I let Kat go," I whispered. "Does that count?"

Were They ever listening when I needed Them?

"Hey there," a woman's voice called out.

I turned to see a park ranger all pressed and proper in her green-on-green attire. "My sister was...here...today...or maybe it was yesterday," I heard myself say. At first her expression registered suspicion, but quickly her face and tone softened, as if she were addressing a small child.

"Here? Today? Well, okay," she said, watching my eyes, studying my movements.

"I think I'm going to fall," I said, feeling the grass slipping beneath my bare feet, forcing me to lean and tilt and finally tumble.

"Whoa!" she yelled, rushing forward. Too late. My face smashed into the fresh-smelling lawn.

After a few silent moments she asked, "Are you ill?"

Dazed and disoriented, I rolled over and forced myself to sit up and focus until the world ceased its dizzy spinning rotations. When all was once again calm, I fixed my sights dead on. "My mother thinks I'm crazy," I said, "but maybe I'm really just sick. I feel sick most of the time, like I'll puke, or my ears will explode, or my head will split, or I'll close my eyes and never be able to get them open...you know. It's scary...you know. Do you? Do you know what I mean?"

She responded simply by saying, "My name's Helen."

"My name is Sandra."

"Sandra. That's a start."

"Sandy."

"Sandy it is. Okay Sandy, do you think you can walk if I help you?"

"I can walk."

"Slowly now. Hold my arm and I'll help you stand. Good."

"Helen?"

"Yes?"

"Just checking. My mind. I have to check things a lot. What did you say your name was?"

"Helen."

"I remember now. Yeah, that's what you said. I won't forget. You said Helen. My name is Sandy."

"Yes, that's what you said. Your name is Sandy."

"I'm trying to keep things in order...so I won't lose them."

"One foot at a time, now. One at a time. That's good. The park office is quite a ways away, so we'll be riding in my car. Can you see the car? Just a few yards more to go."

It was a light green generic car. I kept my eyes on it, aimed for it, and what seemed an eternity later I reached it.

Helen's park ranger office was in a bright building with central air conditioning. There were two men at desks in the middle of the room and the walls were lined with photographs. Old black and white photographs of soldiers. Some were on horses, others marching through ankle deep mud, others holding guns aimed at targets beyond the pictures' borders, and others were lying dead in the fields.

Black and white photographs of boys in blue and grey. I recognized every face.

"I know this battle," I said.

"Battle of Shiloh," one of the men said, staring

curiously at me. I stared back at him until he averted his gaze.

"I was there...today I think...or maybe...yesterday," I said, pressing the palm of my hand against a large photo of the Shiloh Church.

"You sure were," Helen nodded. "That's where we just came from. You remember how you got there?"

One of the men carried a dark green chair to where I stood. He placed it behind me and helped me sit safely, securely, between the confines of its upholstered arms.

"Kat," I said. "Kat wanted to meet all the soldiers I kept running into. Except, sometimes they ran into me. Anyway, I had to take her to meet them because it was time...for her to meet them. Besides, Penny will find her and they will keep each other company. Did you know you can't get there from here?"

"And where's that?" Helen asked.

"There."

"Near the church?"

"No."

All three of the park rangers exchanged confused looks, then looked back at me as if they expected me to explain. But I didn't think I could because somehow I knew they wouldn't understand, and they'd probably decide I was a nutbucket. "My mother thinks I'm crazy," I said.

"I know," Helen said.

"Do you know my mother?"

"You told me a little while ago that your mother thinks you're crazy. What is her name?"

I provided Mom's name and phone number and helpfully added, "But she's probably not home."

"Why do you think that?" one of the men asked.

"She makes clothes for people too lazy to make their own."

"Does she work in a factory?" Helen asked.

"In lazy people's homes. Do you have a bathroom?"

Helen helped me out of the chair and assisted me to a dark green room the size of a closet. She hesitated about leaving me alone, but I pushed her out and shut the door. When I turned toward the toilet my reflection was trapped inside a huge wall mirror hanging above the lavatory.

I swallowed quick and hard, ingested my surprise, and recognized parts of the girl in the mirror, but most of what I observed was frightening. Reaching out, I let my left hand search the wall until my fingers found the light switch. I flipped it up illuminating the three circles of florescent lamp fastened to the ceiling. While jaundiced color filled the small room and fed into the green wall paint, I noticed this person who was me was severely wounded. At least she had been; now her wounds showed efforts of closure. Her right eyelid drooped low on the eye lens and appeared unresponsive in comparison with her left. The left half of her face attempted expressive affects but the right attempted nothing. The sparkle of youth should have radiated from her, yet she could have been a century old. Her flesh crinkled here and puffed there, and she was as fragile and meatless as a decayed carcass.

Life could be tough and she was proof.

And she, I knew, was me.

"Sandra...ah...Sandy?" Helen spoke from the other side of the bathroom door.

"Yes?"

"I've got some lunch. You wanna share a tuna

sandwich?"

"Okay."

I completed my business and did not glance again, even once, at the girl in the mirror. When I exited, the first thing obvious about the office was that both men were gone. Helen seemed to recognize my thought and said, "They went to lunch. I always bring my own. It's cheaper."

"Kat likes...Kat used to like tuna fish and sardines," I heard myself saying.

23

After sharing a lunch which Kat would have heartily enjoyed, Helen allowed me to nap on a cot behind several filing cabinets. I must've been asleep when Mom arrived because by the time I noticed she was there, she and Helen were talking a mile streak like two old friends at the laundromat.

"...thought she was gonna die," Mom was saying, "She fooled 'em. But now with all that's happened, I sometimes think she'd have been better off going like her sister."

"Oh no," Helen whispered, "You don't really mean that."

"Sad thing is," Mom was frowning, "I think I do mean it. It's like raising a six year old all over...and it gets to be a handful...like when she was trying to tear up the floor. Her fingers were all bloody. She just got it in her head she was going to bury that kitten, but she couldn't reason that it would've been easier to bury Kat in the garden. She was trying to tear right through the floor boards, carpet and all!"

Helen sighed, "Maybe she'll get better. I don't know anything about head injuries, but broken bones heal with time. Seems an injured brain would heal. Especially in a kid her age."

"Well, her doctor tells me 'If Sandy doesn't die, she'll live'. I tell you what, doctors charge a lot of money for that kind of expert opinion!"

They both started laughing.

I was off the cot and shuffling toward them before they resumed their conversation. "Mom," I said, "If I don't die, I want to get my horse back. Also, I want another Kat. And I think I need a job. We don't have enough clothes to fold, and we don't get enough mail to decipher. Maybe I could get a job here."

Mom's surprised expression seemed to force all the words out of her mouth.

"I could do a lot around here," I added.

Helen grinned, then asked me, "What would you say to getting a puppy instead of a kitten?"

"I never had a puppy. Yeah. I'd like a puppy, too."

"Wait a minute," Mom said. "We can't afford to buy your horse back. Maybe we could find another cat, but..."

"I'll take a puppy, too."

"I can't buy you a dog," Mom scolded.

Helen whispered to Mom, "My beagle recently had a litter of pups. They're about five weeks old, ready for weaning. I usually sell them. But for Sandy, I'll make an exception. If you don't mind."

"I don't mind," I said. "I'll get one of your beagle puppies. When can I get it?"

Helen glanced at Mom.

"Probably today is a good day," I decided. "I'll get my puppy today. I'm ready to go now." I left Helen and Mom to work out directions to where the puppies would be waiting.

"What's in the box?" I asked. Mom had opened the car door and was carefully placing a shoe box in the far corner of the back seat. Before she had time to reply

I said, "Her name's gonna be Pup! We'll have to make her a doggy bed in my room so I can keep a close eye on her."

"It's a little too soon to be getting another pet, don't you think?" Mom asked.

The question sounded negative so I ignored it. "Pup's a darned good name. Kat would've liked Pup. Fits her real good, don't you think?"

"Sandy, you haven't even seen the dog. I think you're getting carried away with this whole..."

"Kat's with the soldiers at Shiloh," I interrupted.

We drove for several quiet moments before Mom sighed heavily, then spoke. Her face looked tight enough to crack. "One of the other park rangers brought Kat into the office after you left. He said he'd found her inside Shiloh Church."

I stared at the road as it wound snake-like ahead of us.

"That was thoughtful and kindhearted," Mom continued, "taking Kat to a church. I never know what's up with you, what's running around inside your mind. At first it...well I thought you might've...there was rat poison under the kitchen sink." Mom was pulling oxygen slowly into her lungs and holding it before she exhaled. "When I saw Kat was dead...all I could think of was the rat poison. Afterwards I was gonna flush it down the toilet—the poison. But the package was sealed and I realized you didn't kill your kitten. I searched your room and found some tranquilizers under your bed. Kat must've swallowed one. It was an accident, Sandy."

"I didn't hurt Kat."

"No. No, you didn't."

"Kat's with the soldiers."

"Kat's in the box in the backseat."

"Helen has a beagle puppy waiting for me."

"I thought you and me could make a little grave for Kat next to Penny's grave."

"I named my beagle Pup."

"Penny's at Pine Top Graveyard, next to your grandparents."

"Pup's gonna need a warm little bed."

"We'll be there in a minute."

"Kat and Pup would've been friends."

"Penny will keep Kat company, and you can probably walk there from the house. You'll be able to visit both."

"Mom?"

"Yes?"

"I'm feeling sick."

We'd reached Pine Top Graveyard and were entering the small parking space when I vomited on the floorboard carpet. Mom was fast, running around to the passenger door, hoisting me out of the car and steering me toward the lawn. I fell on my knees and barfed until every last morsel of the tuna sandwich was expelled.

"That looks like fish," Mom said.

"Yeah."

"You hate fish. Why'd you eat it?"

"To be polite."

Mom shook her head and smiled while she wiped my forehead with some Kleenex. "Here's a peppermint," she said, unwrapping the red and white candy. "Let it dissolve in your mouth. You can brush your teeth when we get home."

"Okay."

"Wait here. I'll get Kat."

The sun was slipping below the tops of the pine

trees that lined the cemetery when suddenly I recognized this place. It was our family's final rest stop. Penny and I used to come here with our friends late at night. We used to sit on the gravestones and drink beer while we told tall tales, tried to unnerve each other.

"You hold Kat," Mom said, handing me the small box. She carried the shovel we kept in the trunk. "I'll dig the grave."

I was dizzy and nauseated, but the scenario was beginning to make sense. Cautiously I tipped the box top and peered inside. Kat was curled into a peaceful posture. She looked so permanently asleep. I wanted to reach in and touch her fur but something stopped me. It was the memory of a soldier. He was holding her gently upon his shoulder and she was watching me with her round eyes. I could hear her little engine humming.

When Mom returned I handed the box to her. "I want to keep my memory the way it is," I said.

"I don't understand," Mom said.

"You can take this," I touched the box. "I'll go to the car. I won't barf."

"Why...what about...I made a nice little hole in the ground next to..."

"That's good," I cut her off before she could finish. I knew she was prepared to say something about Kat, but I didn't want to listen. There were things I needed to get used to hearing.

"Suit yourself," Mom shrugged and shook her head. I couldn't tell if it was an angry shrug.

24

We traveled the short distance from the cemetery to our house without conflict. Mom parked, ushered me inside and ran a hot bath. "When you're clean we'll get the first-aid kit and take care of your hands. And throw those pajamas away. They're too torn to patch."

I held my hands close to my face and studied the dry blood caked beneath my nails. My fingers were bruised and badly swollen. "Who did this, Mom?"

"You did that to yourself."

"Why?"

"Why?" She threw her head back and gazed at the ceiling while repeating the word why several times.

"Don't you know?" I asked.

She left me alone in the bathroom with a tub full of steamy water, closing the door on me and my question.

After I soaked and scrubbed, I opened the drain and watched with great interest as the water formed a funnel before disappearing. I was fascinated watching how the water did that. Made me think of tornadoes. We had quite a few tornadoes in Tennessee. Penny and I had actually seen one in Memphis. That twister swooped down from the Heavens and ripped roofs from houses just one street away from where we were. I recalled how it overturned cars and trucks, yanking off their hoods, trunks and doors before torpedoing them through brick buildings. I could even remember how Penny and I found a broomstick jammed into a dogwood tree a few yards from where we stood. The broom handle was embedded deep, like a needle in a pin cushion.

We figured it was a miracle we were still standing. Penny knelt and prayed her thank-yous to God and all the Great Magicians for allowing us such a miracle. I was too busy trying to pull the broom out of the dogwood tree.

Hold on!

Just one minute.

Too weird. Don't think about weird stuff, I scolded myself. Too easy to get distracted, and Mom hated my frequent lapses into distraction. She called these occasions my moments of oblivion.

Clean the tub. That was a good practical thing I could do. Didn't remind me of tornadoes or anything.

I found a bright yellow sponge and green scouring powder under the sink, and used these to wipe the white porcelain until it sparkled. The green powder made my fingers burn and sting, but it was a small sacrifice since cleaning the bathtub seemed such a monumentally helpful deed. Mom would be pleased.

When all my tidying chores were finished, I wrapped myself in a burgundy towel and went to my room to find clothes.

A few minutes later I found Mom on the front porch. The porch table was crowded with items: peroxide in a brown bottle, silver tweezers, scissors with pink handles, white gauze, surgical white tape, alcohol in a clear plastic bottle, and antiseptic ointment in a yellow and beige tube.

The colors and details seemed especially vivid to me, as if I were seeing these things for the first time in my life.

"My eyes are acting strange," I told Mom while taking my seat in the empty blue chair next to her.

"What's this green stuff stuck to your fingernails? Smells like chlorine. What'd you need scouring powder for?"

"I cleaned the tub."

"Cleaned it or made a mess for me?" she asked cynically.

"Someone tore the carpet in my room," I said.

"You tore it yourself."

I almost asked her why I would do such a strange thing when I remembered that I'd also asked her why I would shred my own fingers. She hadn't provided reason for that, so I decided to leave it be.

"Hold your hands here," Mom said, indicating a place in midair. When I obeyed she poured peroxide on my hands and fingers. I half expected an uncomfortable sensation but it actually felt cool on my skin.

"Good," she said, "No infection, yet." She removed a yellow towel from her lap and placed it on the tabletop nearest me. "Now put your hands here, palms down."

I obeyed this command quickly and was immediately sorry. She grabbed the tweezers, dipped them in alcohol, and began digging at my flesh in the same way I'd seen her dig potatoes out of the garden using a hoe. Instead of crying out, I gritted my teeth and allowed my eyes to bulge with pain.

This horror continued for ever, or at least until she'd gouged each finger into numbness. All the while I kept hoping and praying she'd see my eyes and know I was dying, but she was too intent on her project.

During the final step she used gauze to generously dab alcohol on my wounds, then finish by applying Band-Aids treated with gobs of antiseptic ointment.

I held my Band-Aid enshrouded fingers before my face to examine them.

"Don't you dare do what I think you're thinking!" Mom commanded.

I was thinking I would go to my room and pull off all the Band-Aids. It was spooky to know Mom could read my mind. Instead of speaking up I leaned heavily into my chair and remained silent while she cleared the table, carrying the contents back into the house.

Mom left me alone to rest on the porch and I must've fallen asleep. When I opened my eyes I realized the sun had set, it was dark and cold, and headlights were easing up our driveway.

"Mom!" I yelled.

No answer.

"Mom! Mom! We've got company!"

That got her attention. She appeared in the doorway wearing her apron, flour dough dripping from her hands.

"See?" I said, pointing at the car which was now stopped in our front yard.

Mom and I watched with curious interest as the car's door swung open and a person got out. It was too dark to see who. The person approached and was walking up the porch steps when I noticed that she or he was making truly bizarre whimpering sounds.

And then I saw why. "Pup!" I screeched, struggling to rise from my chair. My Band-Aid encased fingers were too sore to support my weight and I could feel myself falling backward, slamming my head against the blue chair seconds before my butt slapped the porch.

"Oh my goodness!" Helen yelled, running toward me. Helen set the beagle puppy on the floor before she and Mom simultaneously gripped my elbows and hoisted me back into the chair.

"You got dough all over my arm," I complained, staring at Mom. I'd momentarily forgotten about the puppy. It was at my feet, tugging at my shoestrings.

"Let me explain," Helen was apologizing to Mom. "I didn't bring the puppy to force it off on you, but when I got home from work this evening I couldn't stop thinking about that little kitten, and since you'd told me where you lived..."

"I'm sure you mean well," Mom said, "But I don't think Sandy's...she's not very responsible. She hid some medication. When her kitten got into it...that's how the little cat died."

"I wasn't going to leave the puppy here," Helen said. "I just wanted to show her to Sandy. I was planning on taking her home."

"You don't have to take her home," I said, "I'll keep her." I'd picked the little beagle up and placed her in my lap. She was nibbling at my Band-Aids.

"Sandy! Please!" Mom said. "Don't let her do that! We'll have to change the tape!"

"She isn't hurting anything, Mom."

Mom stared at Helen, a mixture of anger and overwhelm on her face. "I've got chicken and dumplings cooking," she said. "I've got to take them off the stove."

Helen smiled at me reassuringly, then followed Mom into the house.

I could hear them talking about me and Pup, but I couldn't tell much about what they discussed. Fifteen minutes later Mom opened the door and ordered me to get to the table if I wanted dinner.

Carefully I rose from the chair and made my way inside. Pup followed close on my heels. Helen was already seated at the table, which was set for three.

"I've asked Helen to share our meal," Mom said. "You'll like Mom's chicken and dumplings."

"Oh, I can tell I will. Smells delicious."

"Helen's taking the puppy home when she leaves," Mom said.

"Why can't she be home here?" I glanced at Helen for assistance, but she remained silent.

"You're not prepared to care for a pet."

"I am. I took really good care of Kat."

"Kat died because you left your medication out."

"I won't ever do that again," I promised. "I won't. I don't need to take pills, anyway. You can flush them all down the toilet."

"You've got an appointment with Doctor Rheis in the morning, so we'll let him decide that."

"I'll ask him if I can have the puppy," I said defiantly.

"It's none of his business," Mom said.

"Then I'm going to move."

"Really? Where are you moving to?"

While I tried to think up an answer, I ate a few dumplings.

"Your mother said she'd bring you to visit the puppies," Helen said.

"You're going to sell them," I replied with alarm. "How can I visit them if you sell them?"

"I'll save this one," she said, reaching below the table and patting the puppy. "Look how she's already taken to you."

Mom and I bent to observe how the beagle had curled up between my feet and was sound asleep.

After we finished dinner Helen took Pup and left and I retired to my room. It seemed Mom was growing meaner every day.

25

"Follow the orange tape," Mom said.

"What if I get lost?"

"If you follow the orange tape and ignore the other colors, you won't get lost."

"Okay," I said, leaving Mom in Doctor Rheis's reception room. I was on my own in the hospital. Mom didn't think it was a good idea, my cruising through the corridors looking for Unit C where I'd done time. But I wanted to say hello to Blanche. Out of all the nurses, she and the old woman who wore the pinafore were the only two I remembered anything about. Guess they were kind of like friends since I could remember them.

"Watch it!" an orderly cautioned just seconds before I collided with him.

"Huh? Sorry," I apologized. "I have to watch the orange tape," I added to explain why I was staring at the floor instead of looking where I was headed.

"You trying to find Unit C?" he asked.

"No. I'm trying to find Blanche. She's a nurse."

"Blanche Poole?"

I shrugged. I didn't know Blanche's last name.

"You probably mean Blanche Poole. She isn't on Unit C these days; she works in ICU."

"What's that?"

"Intensive Care Unit," he answered.

"Oh. Okay. Well, that's where I'm going. My mom told me to follow the orange tape. It's on the floor." I pointed at the multiple strips of colored tape running side by side.

"Orange goes straight to Unit C," he said. "Blue takes you to ICU, except they won't let you in. No visitors."

"I'll knock on the door and ask for Blanche," I said.

"You're pretty determined to see her?"

I nodded.

"Tell you what, I'll go with you. I can go inside and let her know she's got a visitor."

"Okay." I returned my attention to the tape on the floor, this time stepping across the orange and planting my shoes on the blue.

"Tell you what else," the orderly said, "you keep your head up and watch what's in front of you, and I'll show you how to get there."

"Okay, but you have to walk real slow because I can't go fast, and sometimes I fall. If I fall my mom will be mad."

When we arrived at ICU there were two huge, heavy, blue steel doors that hinged on either side and opened at the center. The orderly asked me to be seated on a sofa in a small room near these double doors. I obliged. The room was empty of people except for me. A television was on showing a daytime talk show, but the volume was turned so low the sound was not audible.

I sat quietly with my hands clasped across my lap for several minutes before I heard the ICU doors swing open. Within seconds Blanche was standing over me exclaiming, "Well, I'll be! I tell you what! That child's doing fine!"

"What child?" I asked.

She chuckled and sat beside me, giving my shoulders a squeeze. "Sandra, dear, you're starting to look like a regular kid."

"I'm not a kid," I said, objecting.

"Well, well," she said, reaching to my face and holding my hair away from my left cheek. "Will you look at that! Very little edema. Not going to be much keloid, either. That's rare in people with your hair and skin tone."

I lifted my hand to my face, remembering the image in the mirror at Helen's park office. I wondered what keloid meant and was afraid it might be another word for ugly.

"I'm going to get a job at Shiloh," I said proudly, wanting to change the topic.

"A job? Why, I'll be! That's great news."

I nodded.

"Wait a minute. What happened to school? Aren't you a senior this year?"

"Mom needs my help at home."

Blanche was studying my eyes and my face.

"My dad left us...and Penny isn't coming home anymore."

Blanche suddenly appeared very sad.

"But we're okay. Me and Mom and..." I started to say Kat, but I caught myself. "We're probably getting a dog. Not a grown dog...a beagle puppy."

"Is your mother here?"

"We have an appointment with the good Doc," I said.

"Then you and me should get you back over there. The good Doc is probably waiting for you."

Blanche walked with me to Doctor Rheis's reception room, but Mom wasn't waiting. The lady at the window told Blanche that Mom was in conference with the good Doc.

"I can't be off my floor any longer," Blanche apologized. "You say hello to your mother. And take care of yourself, Sandra, dear."

I could hear Blanche's white uniform shoes clip-clopping on the hospital's tile floor when she exited. Soon the sounds faded out of range.

Alone and feeling self-conscious, I noticed myself slouching in my chair. Several people seated nearby occasionally sneaked peeks at my face. They probably worried about my keloid stuff and were afraid it was contagious. I hoped it was contagious. I hoped it jumped right off of me and infected their faces, then I could sit smug and sneak peeks at them while enjoying my own little condescending smart-ass smirks.

The lady at the window left her chair and came around a counter which separated her cubical from the waiting area. "Sandra," she called, "the doctor is ready to see you. Would you like to come on back?"

I held the chair's arms and carefully raised up to a standing position. It took a moment to steady myself and make sure my feet were ready to coordinate, one in front of the other, before I made my way across the carpet toward the window lady.

"My mom's still in there?" I asked.

"Yes."

"Okay. Where do I go?"

"Second door on your left. Can you...?"

"Yes," I said, cutting her off.

Mom and Doctor Rheis were seated in the conference chairs nearest the entrance. The chair beside the good Doc was vacant and I immediately sat. My legs were tired from all the walking.

"You're mother informs me you've been taking yourself on some rather wild adventures," Doctor Rheis began.

"No."

"No? What about traveling from your parent's farm up to Shiloh? Wouldn't that qualify as a big adventure?"

"No."

Doctor Rheis laughed and shook his head. "What are we going to do with you, Sandy?"

"I don't know," I said.

He continued to chuckle and shake his head. "You are a miracle child."

"I'm not a child."

"Tell you what your mother and I have decided. We'd like to take you off your medication, except for the occasional antibiotic. I've already written up a prescription for you to take until those fingers heal. How's that sound?"

"I don't like pills."

"No. You sure don't. But you need the antibiotics. We can't risk infections under your fingernails. Promise you'll take them?"

"Okay."

"Good girl! Now. How are your headaches? and how about those earaches?"

"I can't remember."

"When was the last time your head was hurting?"

I shrugged.

"How about your ears? Your mother tells me they've been bothering you a lot. She said you tried to cut one of your ears off. We can't have that kind of behavior, Sandy. We don't cut our ears off just because they're..."

"Vincent Van Gogh did that, not me," I interrupted. I tried to recall when I'd had my most recent pains. "My thinking gets cloudy," I said, trying to explain. "There was a time when my ears and my head almost burst. But I went to Shiloh and watched the soldiers fighting. I forgot about my headache because there was so much blood everywhere...until the one soldier took Kat."

"That's the kitten I told you about," Mom addressed Doctor Rheis.

He nodded without taking his eyes off me. "Soldiers?" he asked. "At Shiloh?" He glanced at Mom. Mom appeared confused.

I decided not to tell them anymore.

"What else happened at Shiloh?" Doctor Rheis asked.

"I met Helen. She is my new friend. I'm getting one of her beagle puppies. And I'll probably go help her at the park office."

"My-oh-my," he said. "You've got a busy schedule planned out for yourself. Tell you what. Your mother and I would like to have one of the teachers from your high school come to your house to give you some tests."

"What kind of tests?" I was suspicious of anyone from my high school.

"Tests to see how well you're doing," he said.

"I.Q. tests, you mean," I said. My high school was fond of giving I.Q. tests. It was their way of controlling people like me and Penny. Too late. They couldn't hold Penny back anymore.

The good Doc chuckled again.

"My eyes can't read," I volunteered.

"Your eyes can't read? Well, well." He stopped

chuckling. "Sandy, turn and look at the chart on that wall." He pointed to an eye chart behind his desk. I could almost see the top two rows, but the strain to view the other rows started my head hurting. I explained this to him.

"Let's have our ophthalmologist check Sandy's eyes," Doctor Rheis said to Mom.

"Today?" Mom asked.

"Let me see if he's in the hospital," Doctor Rheis said, walking to his desk and picking up the telephone.

By the time we left Jackson, I had a full bottle of antibiotics and a pair of eyeglasses. And, the good Doc had arranged for a teacher to meet me at my house in a week to administer an I.Q. test. Mom and Doctor Rheis never confirmed that it was an I.Q. assessment, but I knew. I wasn't as dumb as I looked.

26

The road to the cemetery was steep and tiring, but I managed to reach the gates less than an hour after Mom left. She had gone to Jackson to deliver three dresses she'd sewed for some country club socialite. They were dumb-looking dresses. I told Mom, "A dog wouldn't be seen in clothes as goofy as that."

"Dogs don't wear clothes," Mom said.

I knew dogs didn't wear clothes. Still, if they did, they wouldn't wear stupid things like that.

"Rich people dress weird," I said, seating myself on the ground next to Kat's burial mound.

"Kat, you shoulda seen them things Mom made for that old lady. You woulda lost your sardines."

While I spoke I noticed several weeds had popped up near the small wooden cross Mom made for Kat's grave. Pulling them stained my Band-Aids green. I'd have to put new tape on my fingers before Mom returned; otherwise she'd yell and give us both a sick headache.

"Soon I'm gonna have a new puppy," I whispered, glancing quickly over my shoulder as a car approached. It slowed where the road curved sharp, then resumed its speed and passed by.

"And look at these," I said, carefully removing the eye glasses from my face. "The good Doc wants me to wear these. He promised not to give me pills if I'd promise to use them. It's because of the tests they want me to take. Tests and pills and glasses are all glued together to make the promise. Teachers, too. Somebody...one of the teachers...from my school...is going to visit me at home...I guess."

My thoughts were beginning to stray and the disorganized feeling frightened me. It was new, this sensation of fear. But there was something else lurking behind a dense, heavy curtain. It was that thing that scared me most. I closed my eyes until the screen faded grey, then I opened them and slid my glasses on.

"About the pills," I apologized to Kat, "I'm real sorry."

I had fuzzy recollections of strangers. It seemed like these strangers had more to do with Kat's finding the pills than anything I might have done. Yet, Mom wouldn't approve of my saying that. She would argue there weren't any strangers, and she would threaten to take me back to Doctor Rheis if I didn't agree with her theories.

"Mom's turned into a strange person, Kat. You wouldn't like her very much anymore."

After removing weeds and tidying the area around Kat's tiny grave, I kissed the wooden cross and bowed my head for a moment of silence. This complete, I turned my attention to the much larger resting mound nearby. It had a tombstone with a photograph and inscribed epitaph. These were visible out of the corner of my eye. Once or twice I almost faced them, but I was terrified of the curtain in my mind. I think I was more horrified that someone might throw it open and make me look.

Just then I caught the sound of a familiar vehicle. Glancing up I saw "U.S. Mail" stenciled across the back window of the truck as it rounded the curve and continued off toward my house.

Letters! I hadn't deciphered the addresses on Mom's mail since before Kat went away to that other place. The place in my mind. Of course it wasn't entirely in my mind. I met my new friend Helen in that other place.

Shiloh!

I could remember being at Shiloh and finding a horse.

Or maybe I stole it.

When Penny and I were younger, we found a palomino and a paint hobbled beside a creek.

"Let's cut these hobbles and take these horses home," I said to Penny. "I'll keep the paint and you can have the palomino."

"They belong to someone," Penny said.

"Yeah. Us."

"We can't just steal them," Penny said. "We'll get caught and Mom and Dad will have to bail us out of jail."

"We're too young. The worst we'll get is a coupla days in juvenile detention."

"Tell you what," Penny bargained, "we'll remove their hobbles so they can get around better, but we have to leave them where they are."

To placate Penny, I agreed. Later that evening I returned with a bridle and a rope. It was an easy theft. I rode the paint and led the palomino to our farm, then spent half the night building a makeshift pen in the forest to house my newly acquired stock. Everyday for three weeks I carried water, grain and hay. Early during the fourth week, when I decided to exercise the horses, a neighboring farmer spotted me and phoned the sheriff.

I got four weeks in juvenile detention.

"Kat," I said, "it occurs to me that deciphering Mom's mail keeps me out of trouble. Guess I better go home and do that."

While I worked at rising off the ground another thought came to me, "Remember Mark's letter? Haven't been able to decode all of it. Not yet, anyway." I touched the rim of my eye glasses, "Could be these will help. Well...I'm gonna be going now, but don't worry. You won't be lonely. There'll probably be hundreds of soldiers passing this way today. If not, you got all these folks." I gestured broad to include every resting mound in the cemetery. "These are my relatives. Some been here since the late 1700's. Mostly Indians. I knew all about them once, but I   can't remember. That's okay. They'll introduce themselves."

I turned at the gate and blew a kiss toward Kat's grave, then proceeded plodding down the road.

When I arrived at the mailbox I discovered two letters. As had become my habit, I immediately raised them within inches of my face. Normally, this assisted my eyes in the deciphering process. It wasn't working. Slowly I pulled the letters away until they were at least two feet from my face.

"Sears Roebuck," I read the return address off the first. It came so fast out of my mouth that I repeated the words several times.

"Sears Roebuck. Sears Roebuck. Sears Roebuck. Addressed to Dad. Dad's not here anymore. Better give this to Mom."

Slipping the first letter into my shirt pocket, I confidently turned my attention to the second. "From Mrs—?" There was a name, but my mind did a hiccup and my mouth stumbled.

"Spell it out," I heard myself say. "H-a-w-t-h-o-r-n." I paused to think about the letters. Squinting my eyes, adjusting my glasses and tapping my temples didn't help; despite trying until my brain ached, the word refused to be pronounced.

I breathed a long sigh and decided to let Mom worry about Mrs. Whoever, since it was addressed to her anyway.

Before dropping it in my pocket alongside Sears Roebuck, I held it at arms length. Aha! I could see the outline of a check. "Money for dresses a dog wouldn't wear," I concluded.

When I arrived home, I tossed the letters on the kitchen table before retiring to my bedroom. After seating myself comfortably at my writing desk and arranging my dictionary next to Mark's letter, I noticed green stains on my tape.

Mom would really be mad if I didn't have clean bandages on spotless hands when she got home. Without hesitation I hurried across the hall, peeled the tape off and scrubbed my skin raw. When I'd carefully wrapped fresh Band-Aids around each finger and examined the results, I imagined Mom would never guess about my gardening at the graveyard.

By the time I was back at my desk, I was too tired to tackle my deciphering project. "Sorry, cousin," I said, "but I need a nap."

"Sandy!"

Mom's voice pulled me out of a shallow slumber.

"Sandy!"

I crawled through my sleepy state and shuffled down the hall and into the kitchen. Mom was sitting at the table reading her mail.

"Sears Roebuck," I said proudly.

"Huh?"

"Sears Roebuck."

Mom stared at me for a moment, her face blank, then finally she said, "Oh. You mean you figured out where this came from." She flicked her fingernail against the envelope. "Well. Good for you."

"I woke up," I offered.

"Good for you."

"I was asleep."

Mom paused to glance up at me.

I rubbed my eyes and remembered my glasses were on my desk next to Mark's letter.

"What are you talking about?" Mom seemed distracted.

"I was taking a nap. You woke me up."

"Oh. Go back to bed if you want."

"Why did you call me?"

Mom glanced up again, "I was just checking to see where you were."

"I visited Kat," I said.

"That's nice."

"Did we get a bill?" I asked.

"What?"

"Sears Roebuck."

Mom shook her head and frowned. It wasn't the kind of motion that meant "No, we didn't get a bill." It was one of Mom's "Don't bother me with questions" looks.

"Did Dad get a bill?" I asked.

"How'd you know this was for your dad?"

"I read it. My glasses helped...I guess. Did Dad get a bill?"

"Your dad seems to think he can use his credit card and send us the bill. Where are your glasses?"

"In my room...on my desk. I'm going to get a job at Shiloh," I added helpfully. "I'll pay Dad's bill."

"Whatever," Mom said. She rose from her chair and retreated to her bedroom. I heard the door close hard against the frame.

I picked up the other letter and let a check fall out. Mrs. Whoever paid Mom $275. Next I picked up Dad's bill. The number at the bottom of the column was $300. We were just 25 dollars short. I'd better go see Helen soon and get started working for the park.

Some time later while I was at my desk working on Mark's letter, it occurred to me how easy I'd read the numbers. My eyes didn't get confused and my mouth didn't hesitate in the least. Best of all, I'd figured the difference between $300 and $275 was 25 dollars. It was a snap!

Maybe I'd eventually take over Mom's house accounts. Maybe she'd be pleased if I could do that.

27

"I brought you a little oatmeal with your cream and sugar," I said to Kat while gently setting the bowl on her grave. It'd been several days since I'd visited and it seemed the best apology I could provide was a gift of her favorite treat. As an afterthought I added, "I'm gonna leave this here so you can enjoy it whenever you want."

My fingers were healed and I no longer needed bandages, which was good since there were a dozen new weeds near Kat's cross. I plucked them all and carried their sorry, scrappy, green carcasses to the two foot high stone wall separating the cemetery from the forest.

When I returned, I walked close to the gravestone nearest Kat's little wooden marker. As I passed it I let my hand reach out and brush the cold granite. The icy sensation reminded me of a nightmare as familiar as sweat in summer.

I forced myself to think of recent events. "I had to take a bunch of tests Monday," I said to Kat. "My school sent a teacher. She was at my house half the day. I thought she was gonna move in." The idea made me giggle. "Guess I showed her! She was talking to Mom before she left. She told Mom I had a 'nonverbal I.Q. of 121.' Wow. Big news. She shoulda given me a verbal test. I coulda showed her how to crack secret codes." I smiled again because tests measured zero and were beyond pointless.

"Anyway," I continued, "one good thing came out of it. The teacher told Mom how she could make some money. Today Mom's helping the home-economics teacher with a class full of drippy sophomores. She's showing the drips how to sew a French seam. Geeze, Kat. What's the difference? A seam is a seam. You either sew it up, or you leave it open and you've got a peep hole in your clothes."

I was tiring of listening to myself. "Think I'll go see Helen today. I need to check that park office over and sort out what needs doing. When I get that figured, I'll start doing it and they can start paying me."

As had become my habit before exiting the cemetery gate, I turned and blew a kiss at Kat's cross. Her miniature grave was all but lost in the early morning shadows cast from the large neighboring marker. While I paused, a serious loneliness blanketed me. I grew sad with self-pity thinking that lately all my friends were missing.

Prior to setting a course for the state park, a faint recollection of tuna caused me to pack my own lunch: peanut butter with strawberry jam and four large oatmeal cookies. I'd share the cookies.

Recently I'd discovered Mom's garden boots fit comfortably. Because I had difficulty with laces, Mom replaced the ties with Velcro. I also found a pair of Penny's denim jeans and a long-sleeve gingham shirt to wear. This time I would be dressed appropriately.

As I was preparing to leave, I double checked the soft feather pillow I'd situated in the corner of my bedroom. I had to grin with pride; it was the perfect place for a puppy to nap.

Due to my need to make multiple rest stops and

change course several times when it was necessary to detour around brackish swamps, I didn't arrive at Helen's park office until noon.

"Helen drove over to Pickwick," a man in a ranger uniform said when I entered the office. "My name's Brian. Can I help you?"

"Sandy. That's me. I was here before."

He studied me briefly, then said, "Oh yeah. I remember. You're the girl who left the kitten in the chapel."

"No," I corrected him. "I didn't put her there. I gave her to a soldier. You just found her body. The best part of her was already gone...with the soldier."

Brian stared at me with a dumbfound look.

"I'm gonna eat my sandwich now," I said. "You want a cookie? It's oatmeal. My mom makes them."

"Ah, sure. All right." He cautiously rose from his desk and approached me. I handed him two cookies. "Thanks," he said, taking a bite out of one. "Mmmm howdy! They're delicious."

"Yeah. They are. My mom is a good cook."

"Oh! Now I remember. She came to get you that day. All right. So that's your mother? Real good-looking woman."

I glanced up at him while I chewed my sandwich. "You married?"

"No."

"My dad left us," I said.

"Oh?"

"I'm gonna pay his Sears Roebuck bill."

Brian was staring with that dumb expression again.

"Actually, I'm a pretty good mathematician," I said, thinking how easy I'd calculated that I needed twenty-five dollars.

Brian finished his cookies, but he seemed to be having trouble making conversation.

"My mom is helping a teacher at my high school today," I said, watching his face pain for words.

"She's a teacher?"

"No. Mostly, she works on our farm driving the tractor in the crop fields. When we need money, she makes clothes for snots."

Brian started laughing. "Snots?"

"I meant snobs."

"Same thing, I guess," Brian said. He was still laughing.

"When's Helen coming back?" I asked. Trying to talk to Brian was almost as exhausting as deciphering Mom's mail.

"Well," he checked his wristwatch, "she better be getting here any minute now. I've got to investigate a complaint."

I nibbled my cookies and sipped an orange drink Brian bought from the soda machine. Eventually he slapped a green ranger cap over his curly red hair and grumbled all the way out the door. Helen's tardiness seemed to be depriving him of attending to his complaint. I hurried to the window in time to see Brian drive off in one of the park ranger trucks.

Alone in the park office, I snooped around and wondered what I could work on in my new job. The first time the telephone rang, I answered with, "Helen's desk."

"Hello? Hello? What number is this?" a woman asked.

"This is Shiloh State Park," I said. "What's wrong with you? Don't you know who you're calling?"

"Uh," she said. There was a lengthy pause.
"I'm busy," I said.
"Wait...don't hang up...I'm long distance. Can you tell me what hours the park is open today?"
I glanced quickly around the room and saw a large sign on the wall beside the door. The day-of-the-week bibs Mom made me wear when I was eating had helped me decipher Monday through Sunday. I adjusted the glasses on my nose and concentrated.
"What's today?" I asked the woman.
She paused again.
"Look," I said, "I can't play on the phone."
"Wednesday." The word shot out of her mouth. I surveyed the wall sign. Wednesday 8:00 a.m. - 6:00 p.m.
"Eight to six," I said, adding, "Numbers are easy for me. The sign reads eight to six. I'm sure."
The caller didn't thank me. When I detected a loud click from her end of the line, I set the receiver in the cradle and mumbled, "Rude fruitcake."
By the time Helen returned to the office, I'd answered the telephone five times, and was deeply involved in sorting file folders which were stacked in a messy pile atop the work table in the far corner.
"Sandy! For Heaven's sake! What're...how'd you get here?"
"I walked," I said.
"For Heaven's sake! That's a long walk!"
"Two hours. With seven rest stops and three swamps to circle around."
"For Heaven's sake!"
Poor Helen. She seemed to be stuck on that phrase. I understood how frustrating things like that could be. My mind got stuck on certain words, too. "I'm fixing

these folders," I said.

"Where's Brian? Brian's supposed to be on phone duty! He's not supposed to leave this office!"

"We ate some cookies, then he got mad because he had some complaints."

Helen looked concerned. "He complained about cookies?"

"No. He liked the cookies. Oatmeal. Mom makes them with lots of raisins and pecans. We have a pecan tree. Raisins don't grow on trees. Brian said he had to investigate his complaint. I think he's real mad at you. You guys will probably have a tiff about this."

"For Heaven's sake!" Helen's words were stuck again.

"This corner's a real big mess," I said. "I'm fixing these folders."

"Here! Wait! Let me see what you're doing!" Helen rushed to the work table and began sorting through the three piles I'd started stacking.

"Don't disturb my work," I warned her.

"Excuse me. Now. What is it you're up to? What are these different stacks for?"

I frowned and shook my head at her for being so dense. "Look. These folders have a blue label. These have a green label. And these have a black label. I put blue here, green there, and black is there. Don't touch them."

Helen replaced the folders she'd grabbed. "Aren't you smart," she chuckled. "Blue indicates our office supply invoices. Green is for parks and recreation materials. Black is fish and game personnel, payroll and benefits. We usually just file them all together in the same drawer, but I like what you're doing. This makes more sense. We should have different drawers for blue, green and black."

"Everything needs its own place."

"Right you are," she said. "Well, aren't you smart."

"You already said that."

"I sure did. I already said that. What a smart girl."

Helen was extremely pleased with my job performance. I figured after I'd worked a few times, I'd ask how much she was going to pay me.

28

When Brian returned from his complaint, he and Helen stepped outside for about ten minutes. I took a break and watched from the window near the soda machine. Brian shook his fist at the ground. Helen shook her fist at Brian. Eventually the fist shaking ceased and they began a heated conversation. By the time they came back to the office they were joking and laughing like old buddies.

It made me remember the arguments my mom and dad had with increasing regularity as time passed. I vaguely recalled the day Dad drove off and didn't come home anymore. Too bad they didn't fight like Helen and Brian. Joking and laughing seemed like an excellent way to finish up a good tiff.

"I better start home," I said when the clock struck five. I was moving toward the door, contemplating asking about my puppy.

"Sit down until I finish up here," Helen said. "I'll drive you."

"Where do you live?" Brian asked.

I started to tell him, but Helen interrupted and gave him my address.

"I'll drive you," he volunteered.

"That's a long way out of your way," Helen said, surprised.

"I've got to go to Selmer tonight," he said. "My sister's got some chores for me at my dad's old place."

"Well, there you go. So you'll be passing her farm anyway. If you're sure you don't mind."

"How's Pup?" I asked Helen.

"She's doing just dandy. You want me to bring her to visit you soon?"

I hesitated, thinking how Mom reacted the first time Helen brought Pup to my house. "Can you bring her here?"

"Hmmm. Well, I reckon I could."

"Okay," I said. "Can you bring her Friday? I don't think I can walk back here tomorrow. Mom's gonna be home all day."

"Wait a minute! You mean your mother doesn't know you're here?"

I ignored her scolding tone. "Bring Pup Friday," I said, leaving the office and pulling the door shut behind me. I hurried toward Brian's personal vehicle, a brown and white Ford Bronco. The passenger door was unlocked and I crawled in and buckled my seat belt before Helen could object to anything. I was imagining the feather pillow in my room, waiting for my puppy.

Mom hadn't returned from her new assistant teacher's job when Brian deposited me at my house.

"You're comfortable staying by yourself?" he asked.

"I pretty much stay by myself most of the time," I replied, adding quickly, "That's not a complaint." Brian took people's complaints too serious.

He stalled, "Well, I guess I'll be off then. By the way, you think your mom might drop by the office again?"

I shrugged. Not if I could help it. Mom could be a big complainer when she got started. The thought of what could happen if Mom and her complaints got stirred up with Brian and his problem solving tendencies...geeze!

While Brian drove off down the road, I waited in the driveway and waved until he was out of sight. It seemed the polite thing to do, and I was working at changing my ways. A well-mannered girl with politeness oozing from her pores rested patiently on the fringes of my personality. The idea would shock most people, but I knew such a transformation was possible, if only to make Penny proud of me.

At six o'clock, Mom still hadn't returned. I ate another peanut butter sandwich. Mom seldom phoned to tell me where she was, or when she would be home, and I figured it was none of my business.

Television was monotonous, so I retired to bathe myself, then turn my full attention on cousin Mark's letter.

My many months of effort—plus the new eyeglasses—were paying off. I'd managed to translate most of it, with two and three words often deciphered as quickly as I'd read Sears Roebuck.

Dear Sandy

Got myself in   .   men I saw running   for did   some   .   men   it on me. Wasn't me put stuff in them   .   , the   men. Always get the wrong man. You know how it is kid.

Hey kid, the⁻   won't (write) me, let me know what's up   home. (Write) me a letter, Sandy, keep me   . You know me.   in the   place at the   time. You   ?

Tell your folks, and   Penny, hello. I   to be here in a year. You (write) me. Ain't   gonna. Mark.

I studied my translations until my orbits ached, but couldn't get more than one new word, "write", decoded.

Okay, I thought. That's good enough. The word popped up in three places, which meant I'd cracked the code three times. After fluffing up the pillow that would be Pup's future bed, I crawled under the covers and fell asleep.

Next morning I found Mom seated at the kitchen table, fresh cup of coffee in hand, reading the newspaper.

"Where'd you get a newspaper?" I asked. We'd never subscribed to magazines or big-town newspapers. Mom and dad believed the extra expense frivolous.

"It's the Memphis Commercial Appeal," Mom bragged, spreading the front page for me to observe this fact. "The teachers leave them in their work lounge. I tidied up last night when they left. Your principal told me I'd get paid for all the hours I was there. They owe me for nine hours."

"Are you gonna work every day?"

"Not everyday," Mom said, her tone tinged with a calmness which had been absent recently. "But I'm hired part time. Mostly I'll be assisting the home economics teacher. She told me she could use my help on all pattern, fabric, and stitching assignments. You know, Sandy, for a teacher, she doesn't know much about sewing." Mom was smug and pleased with the teacher's ignorance.

"By the way, young lady. Where'd you go wearing my garden boots?"

"For a walk."

"For a walk," Mom repeated my statement. "Exercise is good for you, but don't let me catch you traveling too far from the house. Are you still visiting Kat—"

she broke off.

"I clean Kat's grave," I said. "The weeds keep crowding her cross. It's not a very big cross, Mom. I think we should get one of those granite markers for Kat."

Mom smiled and, without comment, refilled her coffee.

29

It was one week before Thanksgiving when I completed my sorting and filing project at the park office Helen emptied a three-drawer cabinet that was being used for junk storage and left me to my own devices. I'd transferred my alphabet sheets from my bedroom wall to the wall in the park office above my file cabinet. These helped me keep all the letters in order while I alphabetized the folders before arranging them neatly inside the proper drawers.

On the face of my first file drawer I pasted an index card which I'd colored black. Brian penciled in the words: "Fish and Game Personnel," "Payroll" and "Benefits." On my second drawer I pasted another card I'd colored green. Brian wrote: "Park and Recreation Materials." I colored the third card blue and pasted it on the last drawer. Brian wrote: "Office Supply Material."

"Okay," I announced loudly, "I'm finished."

Helen and Brian made a big display of inspecting my cabinet and fingering through several files, then exclaiming how smart I was. I'd been working an average of two partial days each week at the office since before Halloween, and I'd learned that Helen and Brian were prone to exaggerate their enthusiasm over my duties. This didn't bother me, because I got paid a generous salary.

"Okay," I said, "I'm going home now."

As was my custom, I waited until either Helen or

Brian handed me some money. The sum was always different. When I managed to stay for a full half-day, I'd get five dollars.

"I caught her Tuesday," Helen winked at Brian.

"Must be my turn," Brian grinned. He pulled out his wallet and handed me two five-dollars bills.

I inspected Lincoln's face. "This is too much," I said.

"That's a bonus," Brian said, "for Thanksgiving. After all, we won't be seeing you until after turkey time. Remember? We'll be closed. Anyway, it's a good thing we've got you to help us out since our regular staff gets cut back during winter."

"Okay," I said. "Thank you." I stuffed the bills in my jeans pocket, pulled my coat on, and hurried over to the pen Helen kept for Pup during the days I worked. This time I reached in and picked the little beagle up, cradled her gently in my arms, then addressed Helen. "I'm taking my puppy home."

"You are? Your mom said it's all right?"

I nodded. I didn't want to actually lie to her, but I figured a nod was a silent lie, less likely to be picked up on by Them.

"That's wonderful, Sandy," Helen beamed like a proud mother hen. "Now, do you remember how to feed and water—"

I interrupted, "I always feed and water Pup here. I know what to do. I used to have a kitten, you know."

"That's true. Now, do you remember about her necessary walks?"

"Or she'll poop and pee on the floor," I said, thinking I wasn't the one with the memory problem. Helen forgot I was elected primary caretaker for Pup in the office, and I was the one who always took her for necessary walks.

"You think you'll get too tired carrying her all the way home?" Brian asked.

"I don't need many rest stops anymore," I said. "I go from here to there in one hour, without detours. If I walk straight, it takes too long because of the swamps, and then it really isn't straight."

It required several trial trips, but eventually I stumbled across a quick direct route by simply following a fence line which began at a neighbor's farm and continued almost to Shiloh. Helen and Brian balked at letting me walk home after work, until I promised to always leave by three o'clock. They were afraid it would get dark and I'd get lost, or worse, that I'd get frostbite.

Mom still didn't know about my job at the park. I was saving my money as a surprise to help pay Dad's Sears Roebuck debt. Mom assumed I stayed around the house and visited the cemetery on the days she worked at the school. Guessed I'd have to tell her I was at the park on this day, to explain Pup.

"You want to take some of Pup's kibble chow?" Helen asked.

"No."

"Do you have puppy food at your house?"

"No."

"Tell you what," Brian offered, "I'll drive you home today, that way Pup can ride in my truck, and we can carry all the kibbles. It's a 50-pound bag. That'll save you a few bucks. Puppy food's real expensive."

"Oh. I didn't know it was expensive. Okay. You drive me home and we'll take the whole bag."

"This gal knows a nickel from a dollar," Helen laughed.

Mom's car was already in the carport as Brian

pulled into the yard. "I'm gonna get a headache," I mumbled.

"You have a headache?"

"Not yet. Soon as Mom gets through yelling, then I'll get a headache."

"Uh oh. I've got a sneaky feeling your mom doesn't know you're bringing home a friend."

"You don't count," I said. "She won't get mad because you're my friend. Pup's the surprise."

Brian sighed and grinned while he jumped from the Bronco, walked around to the passenger side and helped me unload Pup and the bag of kibble.

Mom met us half way across the front porch. "Hold it! Just a gosh darn minute, there! Who's this?" She was staring at Brian.

"This is Brian. He's a fish and game ranger, Mom. Brian works with Helen. She's his boss."

Mom cautiously extended her hand in greeting. "Glad to meet you, I think. What's going on?"

"Pleased to meet you, M'am," Brian responded, removing his hat. "I'll set this bag inside your doorway. Sandy, you better do some explaining. Don't get me in the middle of this."

"Pup's gotta have a necessary walk right now," I said, hugging the beagle while hurrying off the porch and around the side of the house.

Pup and I waited in the yard for nearly thirty minutes. When a chill wind settled in and Pup began to shiver, I fortified myself against whatever was to happen and carried my new friend into the house. Mom and Brian were seated in the chairs closest to the warmth from the fireplace. They both sipped from coffee cups and seemed to be getting along well.

"Brian tells me what a big help you've been since

you started working over at the park office," Mom began. Her eyebrows were raised and crooked, but she didn't sound angry.

I seated myself on a stool near them, keeping Pup cradled in my lap. Pup started nibbling on my fingers. "You've been a busy girl," Mom said.

I scratched Pup's head. Brian sat there with a useless grin on his face. Several times I stole looks his way for assistance, but he offered none.

"You better take that puppy to your room," Mom said, "and show her that pillow bed you made for her. She needs to get used to it, don't you think?"

Mom's sudden rush of agreeableness and the strange mellow quality in her voice caused me serious suspicion. I slouched on my stool shielding Pup from her view and waited for the arrows and darts to fly.

"I've invited Brian to stay for dinner," Mom said sweetly. "We're having vegetable soup." She turned to Brian. "They're all from my summer garden."

My gaze traveled back and forth between them, searching for the snag. When it was obvious they'd forgotten me and Pup, and Mom was up to her eyeballs in stories about her work at the high school, I picked up Pup and made my way quietly from the room.

That evening we had an odd dinner. Mom set the table with my dead grandmother's linen tablecloth and matching linen napkins. When I dropped my cornbread into my milk, Mom glared briefly, but Brian thought that was a good idea and dropped his cornbread into his milk, too. Pup was wound up to play, and she raced around the house barking like a wild thing. Mom never said a word about the chaos.

While the three of us slurped homemade soup from porcelain china I'd never been permitted to use,

Mom and Brian talked and laughed. I couldn't recall when I'd last seen Mom enjoy herself.

They completed the evening by making plans for Brian to share Thanksgiving with us.

30

Thanksgiving arrived and Mom asked me to make fruit salad.

"I'll chop up ten apples," I said.

"Try two apples."

"Okay. And you want ten oranges?"

"Two oranges."

"Ten bananas?"

"Two bananas! Sandy, what's with ten?"

"This is a big bowl," I said, lifting the glass container for Mom to note its enormous capacity.

"Two of each fruit will be sufficient," Mom said, wrinkling her eyebrows into a scowl.

"What if Brian eats lots of fruit salad. I should chop ten of everything."

"Sandy! What did I just say?"

I held two apples out for inspection, "Okay, how about this many?"

Mom watched out the corner of her eye while I peeled and sliced the dictated fruit. When my chore was complete I asked, "Can I put pecans in this?"

"That'd be nice."

I carried a measuring glass that held two cups to the basement and filled it with shelled pecans from the freezer. Careful not to spill any, I returned and proceeded to pour the pecans on top of the salad.

"Whoa there!" Mom yelled, grabbing the cup

from my hand. "Here, pick most of these back out. That's way too many."

"I'm doing what you told me," I protested, thinking Mom was really getting on my nerves.

"I'll fix the yams," I said, leaving her with the pecans.

"Pup needs a necessary walk," she said, snatching the yams from me. "Why don't you let me finish with the food, and you tend to your puppy."

Pup tagged close on my heels for several hundred yards. When she thought she'd walked enough, she growled and yapped until I picked her up and carried her the remainder of the distance to the cemetery.

Once inside, I used my hands to sweep yellow and brown leaves away from Kat's grave. The weeds surrendered after Halloween, and now all I had to contend with was falling autumn foliage

For about a month, I'd also been maintaining the neighboring grave. When I first assumed the task the area was overrun with dead weeds and foliage decaying like corpses. Although I would not allow my gaze to fall upon the eyes in the headstone photograph, nor would I let myself decipher the epitaph, the place held a friendliness that never failed to make me feel welcome. Often shaded by the forest, it still seemed blessed with kisses from an eternally warm sun.

Sometimes when I brought an offering of sweet creamy oatmeal for Kat, I also brought a gift for this grave. Once it was a simple bouquet of flowers Dad sent for Penny. Once it was a huge pumpkin I borrowed from farmer John's field, after which I carved the orange gourd and put a candle inside. And once it was a liverwurst sandwich, a plate of chocolate chip cookies and a tall glass of milk.

For Thanksgiving I brought a can of sardines for Kat and I brought three stalks of dried corn tied together with a bright orange and yellow ribbon for Kat's neighbor.

After I opened the sardines and placed them beside Kat's cross, I carefully positioned the corn stalks against the granite marker and arranged them to create a holiday decoration. Penny would've loved it. Penny was the festive one who never tired of creating artistic displays of holiday cheer around our home.

Before I left I dropped to my knees and prayed, "Please God. Please all Great Magicians. Please help my family if You can. And be nice to Kat and all the soldiers. And, if it isn't too much trouble for You, could You say hello to my sister...wherever she is?"

It was the best I could manage in the way of a Thanksgiving prayer. When I gathered Pup, she was running amok through the cemetery, yapping joyous puppy songs. Holding her close to my heart, I turned and blew a kiss at Kat's cross. Then, for the first time, I blew another kiss to Kat's neighbor.

As I walked slowly toward the house, I could see Brian's truck parked in the yard. I was surprised I hadn't heard him drive past the cemetery. Stooping to set Pup on the ground, I felt a stab of pain behind my right ear. The sensation made me dizzy so I sat down.

While I rested in the driveway watching Pup play, a faint memory caused me to think of the pills Mom once forced me to swallow whenever she thought I had discomfort anywhere in my head. For some reason, I recalled what seemed like a television show about terrorists. The pills, the pain, and the terrorists swam in thick fog on the edge of my mind.

The idea of terrorists stuck with me as if they were real. The more I concentrated the more I could see them. I reached out my hands and tried to touch them. I grabbed frantically at the space directly in front of me and forced my eyes to focus.

"Hello," Brian was kneeling and staring at me. "Did you fall?"

"No," I answered. "Where's Pup?"

"Your mother fixed a little plate of turkey and giblets, and she's got Pup in the kitchen scarfing them vittles down right now."

He held out his hand and helped me balance while I got back on my feet.

"Did you see anybody else?" I asked.

"No."

"I thought I saw some terrorists," I confessed and waited for Brian to tell me I was acting crazy. When I told Mom about things like that, she always got mad and accused me of acting crazy.

"I don't do this on purpose," I added.

Brian's face was kind. "Do what on purpose?"

"Act crazy."

"Oh. Well. I reckon none of us act crazy on purpose."

He had my attention and I asked, "Do you act crazy sometimes?"

"Not on purpose," he grinned.

"Me neither," I said. I continued feeling a bit dizzy.

"We'll walk slow," Brian said. "You look pale. You all right?"

"I'm okay," I said. "It's just, sometimes my head feels bad. But don't tell Mom. She'll tell the good Doc and they'll drag them pills up again. Besides, my head doesn't bother me as much as the pills. I think they make me act crazy."

A thoughtful expression overcame him and he responded, "Pills don't agree with everybody. Maybe you're one of them people who just plain has trouble with 'em."

"Yeah," I said, "I guess I am."

In the kitchen, Pup took a brief break from her dish of tasty delights to bounce on my feet and tug at my shoes. Reaching over I scratched her head, then she raced back to her giblets.

Mom had prepared our table once again with good linen and seldom-viewed china. A small roast turkey surrounded by potatoes and corn from our garden was placed in the center of everything. Two small pies, one pumpkin and one pecan, were displayed on the counter beside a fresh pot of coffee.

"I made the fruit salad," I announced, pointing at the conspicuous bowl.

"I do enjoy a good salad," Brian said while surveying the spread with approval.

Mom crossed the floor to inspect my hands. "You're a mess," she scolded. "Go wash up, and change your clothes. Where do you find all that dirt?"

"Guess I just get lucky," I mumbled under my breath.

Mom didn't hear. She was busy pouring coffee for herself and Brian, and bragging on about how light and flaky her pie crust turned out.

While I was in my bedroom changing clothes, Pup trotted in and plopped on her feather pillow. From the amount of gastric noises belching from her orifices, I figured she needed a few hours to sleep off her feast.

When I returned to the kitchen, Mom and Brian

were seated, absorbed in conversation while sipping their brew. I pulled out my chair, sat and arranged my linen napkin politely on my lap. I seriously hoped They were watching. I felt changed. Reformed, you might say.

Suddenly Mom turned her attention to me, "Sandy, we'll begin with a nice prayer of thanks." She emphasized the word nice.

"Okay."

Mom raised her eyebrows.

"What!" I said, checking my hands and fingernails to be sure they were clean.

"Will you say the prayer?"

"I already prayed today," I said.

"We're waiting," Mom said. Her left eyebrow was beginning to arch while a fingernail tapped her saucer.

This is really going to confuse Them, I thought. I was not one to pray twice under the same rising sun. "Let's bow our heads and close our eyes," I began. When Mom and Brian had done this, I kept my eyes open and kept my head high. Next I said, "Dear God and dear Great Magicians. Don't be taking this too personal, but I want to ask Your blessings again. Bless Brian for being a good friend to Mom. Bless Mom for being my Mom. Bless Pup because I love her very much. Bless Helen for being my friend. And take good care of all the rest of my family, wherever they are. Oh, and bless this turkey for letting us eat him. Amen."

Mom opened her eyes and smiled proudly at me.

Our dinner proceeded with peaceful calm, and was filled with friendly stories from Brian and delicious food from our table.

For once I was almost safe, protected from the pills and terrorists and cannon fire. Except for the curtain concealing things from me, I might have felt comforted.

31

It was two p.m., four days before Christmas. Brian had claimed something he called comp time and was already gone. He confided to me that he was buying Mom a new sewing machine, one with a cabinet full of accessories. Brian and Mom had spent considerable time together since Thanksgiving, and he was taking her out for dinner and dancing at the Sheraton in Memphis for New Years Eve. Between her assistant teacher's checks, and the money she made sewing clothes for socialites, she'd been able to buy herself a remarkable arrest-me-red evening dress and crimson satin high heels for the occasion. It was one of Mom's quirks. As an expert seamstress, she could've sewed anything she wanted, but Mom seldom made her own clothes.

When Brian boasted about the new machine he was giving her for Christmas, I almost told him she'd rather have something frivolous, something pretty.

When Dad was home, they never believed in frivolous.

Sometimes I wondered if Dad was ever coming back. I heard Mom tell Brian she was getting ready to chuck his clothes out on the highway. She also said she was cancelling his credit cards. That reminded me of the Sears Roebuck bill. I tried to imprint the bill on my mind's memory board because it seemed like my last link to my dad. I worried what would happen if Mom cancelled his cards. I worried he'd never send Penny flowers again. I considered how lovely the flowers looked when I used them to decorate the graves.

"C'mon, c'mon, let's get a move on," Helen sang, snapping her fingers. "Soon as we're through, we're out of here till next year."

Our office closed at two-thirty and would remain closed for the holidays until after New Year's.

"I finished all my folders," I said. "After I clean Pup's pen and wash her dish, I'll be ready to go shopping."

"Sounds like a winner," Helen said.

Helen had promised to take me Christmas shopping. It was the first day I'd worked that I decided to leave Pup at home. I knew we couldn't expect her to stay in Helen's car while we shopped. Cleaning up her things made me sad. It was a new sensation, one I wasn't used to feeling, and it clung to me like a rash. It was there when I woke up, and it was the last thing itching at me before I fell asleep each night.

Pup was a comfort, as were my visits to the cemetery. Still, I couldn't shrug this gloom off my shoulders. When I told Brian about it, he'd assured me it was a stage I had to endure until it was ready to pass. "It's all part of losing," he said. "Losses are painful. Time's the only thing that can help you."

I knew about losses, but I didn't relish the idea of enduring anything.

"Well," Helen said while we fastened our seatbelts, "Where do you wanna go when we get to Jackson?"

"Sears Roebuck," I said without hesitation.

When we passed through Sears' main entrance, several people turned to stare rudely. Helen and I stared back until they averted their beady little eyes and found other obnoxious ways to spend their sorry lives.

"Don't pay attention to these dim wits," Helen winked. "Guess they're just not used to seeing two girls as pretty as you and me in the same room at once."

"I guess not," I said. My hands touched the raised scars on my face and I tugged to make my hair fall over my cheeks.

"Where should we go first?" Helen asked. "How about perfumes? You can buy your mother a nice fragrance."

"No. I'm going down the escalator."

"Downstairs?" Helen was surprised. "Nothing down there except credit and gift wrapping. We can't get wrapped what we haven't yet bought."

"I need to pay on my dad's bill," I said.

"Oh?"

I made my way through children's toys toward the escalator. Helen followed close on my heels. When I arrived at the credit window and asked for my dad's bill, the clerk avoided looking at me. She kept her gaze on the counter. "What's his account number?" she asked.

I reached into my pocket and pulled out some cash. "I don't know, but I want to make a payment."

"No account number?" By now she was surveying her multi-ringed fingers. "That might take a while. What's his full name?"

I provided this information and she hurried into another room. When she returned she said Dad's credit account had been paid in full and was now closed. I reluctantly stuffed the cash into my pocket.

"Okay," I said, turning from the window. Helen remained silent the entire time, but she wasn't much of a poker player. "Don't feel sorry for me," I said.

Helen shrugged slightly, then followed me up

the escalator.

My dad was gone forever. I imagined Mom strewing his possessions across the highway somewhere in Tennessee. It was a cold lonely thought and it made me shiver.

"I guess I don't need to buy him a Christmas present," I said while we walked through the men's clothing department.

Helen's sad droopy eyes studied my face, but she didn't respond.

"I know!" I said, getting a fresh idea. "I'll buy Pup new bowls, and a giant rawhide toy, and a collar with some of them rhinestones! Just like diamonds. She'll really like that!"

"Oh my. That could be expensive."

"I've got twenty-five extra dollars," I said.

Our first visit was to the pet department, where I purchased everything exactly like I'd said. For Kat, I included a pretty pink feline collar. Next, I selected a pair of brown leather driving gloves for Brian. Helen remarked that Brian would love them. My last stop was in the women's nightwear department.

"You go mind your own business," I instructed Helen. "I'll meet you back where the toys were."

Helen frowned. "I don't think I should leave you..."

"Mind your own business," I repeated.

Helen reluctantly made herself scarce. I browsed for a short while, then decided on a box of delicate white lace handkerchiefs for Helen, and a soft powder-blue flannel night shirt for Mom. Mom loved warm flannel in the winter, and blue was her favorite color.

As I was leaving this department, my gaze fell upon a pair of beautiful hair combs. Penny would've absolutely loved these. I used my last eight dollars to get them.

When I found Helen in the toy department, I handed her the boxed handkerchiefs.

"What's this?" she asked.

"Merry Christmas," I said. "I don't have any money left to wrap them, and after you take me to my house, I won't see you until January."

Helen gave me a mother-bear hug that was embarrassing.

"Thank you for bringing me shopping," I added.

She hugged me again. I was about to thank her for being my friend, but decided I'd had enough hugs for the day.

32

On Christmas Eve morning, I used Mom's garden shears to cut a bough from one of the pine trees in our yard. With Pup racing out ahead announcing our journey, I made my way to the cemetery. I carried the bough, a small bag of ornaments, and a cranberry-pinecone-popcorn wreath that I'd made the day before.

I dug a hole and planted the bough between the two graves, and then I carefully decorated it to create a Christmas tree. When I was finished, I hung the wreath around the top. Pup had been preoccupied with noisy activities when suddenly she halted at my heels and stared in silence at the tree.

"We should pray," I said, scooping her into my arms.

"Dear Miracle God. Dear Great Magicians. You really are very good miracle magicians. Thank You for helping me. I know You are taking good care of all the soldiers. I know You are giving Kat lots of good things to eat. But especially I know You are happy to have Penny in Heaven because she is the best person I ever knew."

My eyes left the beautiful tree and traveled beyond the curtain to the photograph. My sister's large dark eyes smiled back at me. I reached out and touched the long black braids which fell across her shoulders. Slowly I dug into my pocket and pulled out the exquisite hair combs. Kneeling, I placed them at the base of her splendid granite headstone.

"Merry Christmas," I said, bowing my head.

Before I left, I hung the pink feline collar over Kat's cross, and I blew great big kisses everywhere.

Later that evening, Mom and I decorated a small tree which she'd purchased in town and set up in our living room. Mom made popcorn candy and hot chocolate. When Brian arrived, we plugged in the lights and watched them blink off and on. We shared presents and Pup stole all the ribbons and ran through the house distributing them everywhere.

Before I retired, I decided to ask for help.

"Brian," I began, "I have a letter. It's from my cousin."

"Which one?" Mom asked.

"Mark."

Mom scowled.

"Anyway," I ignored her, "I have Mark's letter in my room. I've been trying to decipher it for a long time. Will you see if you can figure out what it says? There are only a few words left. I deciphered most of it already."

Brian shot a brief glance at Mom, then said, "Sure. Bring the letter here. Let's see what we can do with it."

Brian examined Mark's code language for a few minutes. When he looked up at me he said, "I believe I've got it figured out. You want me to read it?"

I nodded.

"It says:

'Dear Sandy:

'Got myself in prison. Coupla men I was running packages for did some dirt. Badge men pinned it on me. Wasn't me put stuff in them packages. Ass holes, the badge men. Always get the wrong man. You know how it is kid.

'Hey kid, the family won't write me, let me know what's up around home. Write me a letter, Sandy, keep me posted. You know me. Just in the wrong place at the worst time. You understand?

'Tell your folks and cousin Penny hello. I expect to be outa here in a year. You write me. Ain't nobody else gonna. Mark.'

"So that's why Mark's in Florida," I inhaled deeply. "Alligators down there. I don't like Florida."

"Your cousin's been dealing drugs." Mom sounded harsh.

"Bad road to be on," I said, suddenly getting a picture in my mind of horses fleeing, cannons firing, and soldiers dying as far as my eyes could see. "Not me. I'm gonna be a mathematician, or something like that. I'm good with numbers."

Mom looked at Brian. "She is pretty darned good with numbers," Brian said.

I took my letter from Brian.

"You keep your distance from Mark," Mom said.

"Mark needs his family," I said. "Otherwise, he might meet the soldiers."

For once, Mom was speechless.

"Good night," I said. Pup hurried down the hall ahead of me, yipping and yapping.

33

Christmas morning arrived. I rose early and packed my writing tablet, pencil, eraser, and dictionary into Penny's weathered and worn plaid satchel.

To avoid waking Mom, I quickly carried Pup outside before she had time to announce things. It was overcast and cold, with snowflakes spitting winter kisses from Heaven.

When I reached the cemetery I greeted Penny and Kat before dusting snow off our little tree's wreath. Then Pup and I snuggled comfortably midst our family while I attempted to compose my letter:

"Dear Mark,

"I'm sorry you're in prison. You could say I've been in prison, too. But now I'm busting out...."

Joan Leslie Woodruff is of mixed Native Merican ancestry and lives in the Manzano Mountains amidst the ancient Anasazi ruins where she owns and operates a cattle ranch. The recipient of advanced degrees in health care and education, Ms. Woodruff worked in several major hospitals in California for fifteen years before returning to her native New Mexico to write fiction. Her first novel, *Neighbors,* concerned the spiritual life she discovered living beside the ruins of the prehistoric American cliff dwellers.

Ms. Woodruff has published widely both in literary magazines and health-care journals. *The Shiloh Renewal* is her second novel.